An Unwordly Weatherman
The Highs and Lows of
Bill Foggitt

by

Michael Cresswell

**White Rose Books
& Hutton Press Ltd.**
2000

Published by

White Rose Books
79-81 Market Place, Thirsk,
North Yorkshire YO7 1ET

and

The Hutton Press Ltd.
130 Canada Drive, Cherry Burton,
Beverley, East Yorkshire, HU17 7SB

Printed and bound by
The College Press,
a division of the University of Hull

ISBN 1 902709 07 1

Contents

Page

Author's Notes 4

Foreword by Bob Rust 5

Introduction 7

Chapter 1: Foggetts or Foggia-ites
A Surgeon's Search for the Truth 12

Chapter 2: Buried in Thirsk: The Woman
who went down with the "Titanic" 16

Chapter 3: A man of God - and the Gun 27

Chapter 4: A Young Man's Fancy lightly turns
to Thoughts of Love 51

Chapter 5: Army Life: Private Foggitt muddles through 59

Chapter 6: A Doomed Marriage 73

Chapter 7: The Concrete Jungle 80

Chapter 8: A Painful Introduction to a new Career 92

Chapter 9: Banana Skins and a disastrous Love Affair 113

Author's note

Researching family backgrounds can be a thankless task, requiring infinite patience and an ability to rise above occasional bitter disappointment as promising leads disappear into genealogical blind alleys.

For more than twenty-five years, Dr Paul Foggitt has been delving into parish registers; reading venerable books, and perusing hundreds of documents to produce a comprehensive record of the Foggitt family, dating back as far as 1484, and in so doing has succeeded in bringing forgotten forebears back to life.

And his work is far from over. Many more facts need to be ascertained before he can say with certainty that he has accomplished what he set out to do, but the tremendous amount of information he has already uncovered, would, I am sure, be worthy of a book in its own right.

Disproving a family assertion that a wife had gone down with the Titanic, when she, in fact, deserted her family and ran away to London with a paramour, was just one of the multitude of challenges he overcame.

Dr Foggitt has kindly allowed me access to such information as I deemed necessary to the story of his distant cousin, Bill Foggitt, Britain's most famous amateur weather forecaster.

For this I am deeply grateful as this, together with certain photographs he lent me, have proved invaluable in filling several historical gaps, and giving greater authority to this account of Bill's progress through life.

I am also extremely grateful to Claire Strafford and Hildegard Hodgson for their valuable help in preparing the manuscript, and to Harry Mead, author of 'Inside North Yorkshire' for allowing me to reproduce the excerpt about Sir Thomas Chalinor and alum industry.

Michael Cresswell

Foreword

While at Yorkshire Television, Bob Rust appeared alongside his amateur colleague on numerous occasions, and their lighthearted banter about their respective methods of forecasting struck a chord with millions of viewers.

He recalled: "Bill Foggitt first came to my attention about thirty years ago. At that time I was working for the Meteorological Office as a weather forecaster at Bawtry. I suppose he was then regarded as 'the enemy.' Here we were in the Met Office, using all the latest scientific technology to try and predict the behaviour of the weather for two or three days ahead, when up popped this chap who had the audacity to say he could forecast the weather for up to six months ahead, by studying the behaviour of moles and midges. Outwardly we regarded Bill as just a "nutter", but deep down we were very concerned. The longest period forecast we produced was a rather poor forecast for a month ahead. In many Met Offices throughout the country, Bill's forecast was pinned to the notice board and we all breathed a sigh of relief if it went wrong. We were approached many times by the media to comment on Bill's latest predictions but we were under orders to make no comment.

The name Bill Foggitt became nationally known and he became a regular face on Yorkshire Television. It was somewhat ironic that years later I was to become the weatherman on Yorkshire Television, in a way taking over Bill's spot. However, his services were still retained and he was often called in to give one of his long term predictions. This gave me the opportunity to meet Bill and I was somewhat surprised to find that he was just a very quiet, pleasant gentleman, hardly the sort of person to have the Met Office quaking in their shoes. I met him on many occasions after that and I often would refer to Bill, or some of his strange forecasting methods, when I did my presentations, so in a way he used to be a source of material to me. I have interviewed Bill on occasions and often taken him to task about his forecasts but we never fell out. He would just sit there and smile. He was probably thinking, "I'm better known than you are, Bob Rust." This was a fact, and from the many people I have met, the name Bill Foggitt is held in high regard. Let's face it, it is far more magical when Bill predicts the weather, using signs in nature, than when Bob Rust talks of highs, lows and isobars.

Things I will always remember about Bill Foggitt are that he always preferred a pint to a cup of tea, and he was such a quiet, pleasant person.

One final, amusing tale was when he appeared on television along with an expert on fungi (toadstools, mushrooms, etc). Bill was sitting next to this chap and started up a conversation by saying that there were a lot of moles around this year. The fungi man misheard him and thought he said there were "a lot of moulds around." He responded to Bill by agreeing and elaborated by saying they were in many colours and some were even red with spots on them. I will always remember Bill's perplexed look; he really had never heard of multicolored moles with spots. I think that this story demonstrates Bill's affable and believing personality."

Foreword by Bob Rust, a senior forecaster with the Meteorological Office for 37 years, who appeared on Yorkshire Television for 13 years, during which he made more than 10,000 predictions, and won the Sony 'Personality of the Year' award in 1988/9.

INTRODUCTION

Before his more famous neighbour, James Herriot, who lived in a village about five miles away, struck an environmental chord with millions through stories based on his veterinary experience, Bill Foggitt of Thirsk, North Yorkshire, was establishing his reputation as a weather prophet, relying on priceless family records dating back to the early part of last century, an old aneroid barometer, and the super-sensitive nature of plants, animals, insects and birds.

Like Herriot, better know to local people as Alf Wight, Bill has achieved national and international fame - although not on the same scale - through his quirky, homespun methods of forecasting, which from time to time have confounded meteorological office experts with all their multi-million pound technology.

For instance, in 1968, he predicted with astonishing accuracy, the whole of the forthcoming winter, virtually week by week - a feat which it is highly unlikely even the most seasoned media weatherman would attempt.

In some ways Bill resembles Herriot. A modest countryman, he has never sought anything more than a contented home life; not to place himself on a public pedestal, despite the attentions of television, radio, newspapers and magazines.

He is not, however, quite as jealous of his privacy as his contemporary.

He shares with the late vet an intense love of nature, dating back to boyhood walks on Sunday afternoons with his mother and father. The wonders they explained to him were later to inspire his thoughts and theories.

Herriot put cows before computers and brought his country characters to life in a warm and understanding way.

Bill presents his friends of the wild in a less personal way, but with equal empathy.

The wonderful animal characters created by Beatrix Potter and Kenneth Grahame are not all that far removed from Bill's frogs and moles, which differ however, in that they are anything but creatures of fantasy.

In the weatherman's case they appeal to a more adult audience, and have played an important part in his predictions: frogs by their spawning habits, and moles through their tunnelling activities.

But it is his records, started in 1830 by his great-grandfather, Thomas Jackson Foggitt (1810-1885), and continued by his grandfather, uncle and father, before being taken over by Bill in 1967, which are the source of his in-depth knowledge of weather patterns.

Sadly, the great compilation of facts and figures, a monument to the dedication and determination of past generations, which has enabled Bill to provide answers which have startled professional meteorologists, has now suffered grievous depredations related directly to his failing eyesight. It is believed that a large part of them may have been thrown out by a woman cleaner he once employed.

He was the first member of his family to "go public" with these meticulously-kept annals which because of the weather patterns they contained, were particularly useful in long range forecasting.

Yet surprisingly it was not so much the Aladdin's Cave of reliable data which shot Bill to fame, so much as the apparently purposeless behaviour of plants, animals, birds and insects, which he interpreted to a credulous public as being entirely due to varying weather conditions.

And, bored by concrete and computers, and an increasingly regimented way of life, people swallowed this all-but-forgotten nature lore in huge draughts.

The Press quickly realised that this colourful new world represented an exciting alternative to the daily round of mundane "diary" stories. Following his "discovery" by the Yorkshire Post in 1968, Bill was snapped up by the newly-established Yorkshire Television to add lighthearted comments to the official weather forecast, "as a bit of a gimmick."

The "gimmick" was remarkably successful, and Bill rapidly established himself as something of a cult figure - the archetypal rustic in a tweed overcoat and deerstalker hat, proffering advice based on the behaviour of seaweed and pine cones.

He took to television like a duck to water, and went down with viewers like a draught of homemade wine. He stayed with YTV for 15 years, during which time, he said, the official weathermen were extremely kind towards him.

"Bob Rust, in particular, chatted to me and put me at ease. He was full of humour and lighthearted banter when he interviewed me. His very presence gave me confidence, although we approached the weather from different sides of the fence. I remember he came up to Thirsk one, and I said I was ready for a pint, but Bob told me that first we would see what local people thought about me.

Old Tom Charlton (he recently died aged 100) said I was a gentleman, but didn't comment on my weather prophecies, and a woman replied that she didn't know about my predictions, but I was a "lovely man".

Then we went to Thirsk School. I never got my pint! It was typical of Bob that once, before interviewing me about my methods of weather forecasting, he winked at me and told me not to take any notice of his gently provocative questions - it was the way the programme wanted it.

Then he went on to say, 'Now Bill, you're not telling me that moles can tell what the weather is going to do, are you?'

Afterwards he grinned and told me he fully believed what I said."

Of course, Bill had his detractors, who sneered at his methods and labelled him a country crank, but he learned to live with - and even enjoy - criticism, for most of it was delivered in a kindly way.

However, many thoughtful viewers saw the wisdom of his predictions and theories, and were delighted when he put one over the experts. They were intrigued by the mysteries of nature as Bill unfolded them, and by weather sayings which had their origins hundreds of years previously.

Later, as his reputation grew, Bill was to acquit himself honourably in contests with professional meteorologists, arranged by newspapers.

Editors were by this time constantly despatching reporters and feature-writers to his gloomy home, South Villa, Thirsk, with instructions to turn in "colour" pieces about the quirky weatherman.

And Bill would always oblige, sending them back to the city with fascinating stories about plants which went to sleep at noon; of frogs that presaged dry weather by depositing their spawn in the deepest part of a pond; of moles which foretold the end of droughts, or Arctic spells, or of lazy flies attaching themselves to the human body when thunderstorms were in the offing.

But it was in 1985, when he was 71, that Bill finally hit the big time and found himself unexpectedly catapulted onto the international stage. The Met. Office had told the nation to expect a continuation of the current bitterly cold spell, but the Thirsk sage noticed a mole poking its nose through the snow, and asserted that warmer weather was due the following Thursday.

He was spot on - and at last the world began to take Bill Foggitt seriously. There was obviously more to his way of forecasting than they had believed.

Overnight this modest countryman, whom many reckoned made his predictions on the basis of trial and error, found himself lionised, and sought after by film crews from the USA, Japan and Germany.

Soon he was taking the train to London at least three times a year to appear on television and radio.

Folksy Foggitt had become factual Foggitt. For a short time he wrote an "alternative" weather column for the Daily Mail.

Academic recognition came in 1993, when he contributed some of his observations of nature to a science publication for the national curriculum, produced by Reading University.

The professor who directed the project later described Bill as a "living legend".

But perhaps one of Bill's most significant achievements has been to join other notable conservationists in making the general public more aware of the importance of nature in the world about us, for people must surely realise that the instincts and sensitivities of plants and tiny creatures entitles them to new respect and consideration.

Fortunately we live in an environmentally-friendly age in which the preservation of wild life is being pursued in a vigorous and sympathetic way.

Now in his twilight years at 86 years of age, Bill's eyesight is failing and he can no longer read the records, but in Mrs Betty Cook he has a devoted housekeeper who will do this for him, and who has taken over monitoring the rainfall and temperature figures which the family has supplied to the meteorological office for over eighty years.

Bill is totally guileless and generous to the point of naivete, as an unfortunate encounter with a "femme fatale" in 1984 bore out.

His father once told him that if ever a con-man appeared on the doorstep, he would probably depart with the deeds to South Villa, if Bill had anything to do with it, and it is with this sobering recollection in mind that his son now has a "hot line" to the police.

To Bill, "streetwise" means negotiating the busy main roads to and from Thirsk with the aid of a white stick. He sees no ulterior motives in his fellow human beings, and has an enviable ability to laugh at himself and his mishaps.

A belief that "Someone up there is looking after me" has been a sure shield against the pitfalls of life.

Even his marriage, 52 years ago, which was never dissolved, faded away without any rancour or messy legal proceedings. He only saw his wife once after they separated, and admits that on occasions he feels a mild sense of guilt and sadness that things didn't work out between them.

Despite his strict Methodist upbringing, however, and the fact that he has been a local preacher in the church for more than 60 years, Bill doesn't have any sense of self-reproach about his liking for a pint of beer a day, or after taking a Sunday evening service.

He particularly enjoys the company of his "magic circle" of friends at two of Thirsk's more genteel hotels, who comforted him after his 1984 debacle.

In this book I have tried to outline the major events in Bill's life, based on a friendship which started while I was covering Thirsk area for the Darlington & Stockton Times.

During that time I was closely associated with him in many of the "situations" in which he found himself, and was sometimes able to help in a small way.

In fact at one time I had the idea of compiling his mishaps in a short, easy-to-read booklet of only a few pages, but as we talked, the story of his life constantly interposed, with the inevitable result.

Bill's quirky observations of nature, in conjunction with old country sayings have appeared in three previous books, 'Bill Foggitt's Weather Book', 'Weatherwise' and the 'Yorkshire Weather Book', and for this reason I have avoided over-concentration on a subject which has also been exploited to the full by television and the Press.

This is an account of a truly selfless man who, despite his many disappointments and limited means, has always declared: "I have been richly blessed."

CHAPTER 1

FOGGETTS OR FOGGIA-ITES ... A SURGEON'S SEARCH FOR THE TRUTH

The history of the Foggitts has been meticulously researched and documented over the past 25 years by Dr Paul Foggitt, a distant cousin of the weatherman, who worked as an orthopaedic surgeon at Burton-on-Trent, and is now living in retirement at Ripon.

He has filled several volumes with detailed accounts of the activities and achievements of the family, and produced a genealogy which, when fully extended, stretches for 45 feet.

One of the reasons which set this remarkable feat of literary detection in motion, was a desire by Dr Foggitt to prove or refute a contention, commonly held in the family, and particularly so on Bill's side, that the original Foggitts emigrated to this country from Foggia, in southern Italy, in the 16th century, because, being Protestants, they were fleeing from the wrath of the Pope.

The theory holds that the newcomers settled in the Cleveland district, where they found work in the alum mines, and became known as Foggia-ites, which was quickly abbreviated to Foggitts.

It sounded a reasonable enough assumption, especially as Bill's great-grandfather, who was born considerably nearer that era, apparently used to support it.

However, Dr Foggitt was far from convinced, and set out on his long journey into the past. Gradually, certain pieces fell into place, and his research revealed Foggitts as far back as 1484, scattered all over Northumberland, Durham and Holy Island, predating the supposed emigration by anything up to a century.

Of course, in those days, there were variations in the spelling of their names, such as Fogart, Foggard, Fougart, Foggett and Forgott, but his was put down to the fact that in those days, most people were illiterate, and their names were recorded by parish incumbents as they were pronounced.

Dr Foggitt stresses, however, that they had no connection with the Froggatts, who originated in North Derbyshire.

The name Foggett has its origin in agriculture, a foggett being a pasture where grass was grown for the winter, which presupposes that the ancestors of the family were farmers, or labourers engaged in this occupation.

Over the centuries, generations of the Foggett clan drifted south into places like Yorkshire, and the spelling of their name changed to Foggitt.

Until recently, Dr Foggitt thought the Foggitts of Thirsk derived from his own ancestors, John Foggitt and Ann Bulmer, who married and lived at Warlaby, near Northallerton in 1662, but this is now in doubt.

John's descendants were later engaged in the woollen industry, centred on Snape, near Bedale, until its demise led to it becoming centred on Leeds and Bradford.

On Bill's side of the family, it is beyond doubt that Thomas Foggitt, believed to have come from South Shields, married Ann Jackson in 1802, and on the deaths of Ann's parents, took over the running of the Blue Bell Inn, at Egglescliffe, across the River Tees from Yarm, of which Mr Jackson had been the publican since circa 1770-5.

It seems that Thomas Foggitt combined his trade with farming, since the 1841 census, taken when he was 60, described him as a farmer. In the 1851 census, however, he was described as a retired blacksmith.

The coaching inn still occupies its commanding location on the slope overlooking the River Tees, and the land leading down to the river is still known as Foggitt's Banks. The inn, which has recently been completely refurbished, undoubtedly has one of the finest positions of any public house in the district.

Ann died in 1851, following a bad fall, and her husband survived her by only three years.

Between them they produced four children, one of whom, Thomas, died in infancy, but the other three carved out prestigious careers for themselves. James, born in 1802, became postmaster at Yarm, where his other interests included tea dealing, patent medicines, book-selling, book-binding and printing.

His former home is now occupied by the NatWest bank.

The second son, Thomas Jackson, Bill's great grandfather, was born in 1810, and it was his interest in meteorology and natural history which became the inspiration for a more scientific approach to these subjects by succeeding generations, thus creating the Foggitt "dynasty" of amateur meteorologists, botanists and orthithologists, which brought them national recognition.

Thomas was educated at Yarm grammar school, and originally intended to become a medical student, but was struck down by typhus at the age of 16, which weakened him considerably and resulted in his transferring to pharmaceutical studies.

However, a more bizarre explanation, espoused by his great grandson, Bill, is that he changed course simply because he could not stand the sight of blood.

After training in pharmacy in York and Portsea (Portsmouth), he became manager of a shop in Chester for five years, before returning to Yarm, where he set up his own business.

Two years later, in 1836, he decided to expand, and was persuaded by a friend to move to Thirsk, where he took premises in the market place.

For a while the two chemists shops ran side by side, and Thomas is said to have regularly walked 20 miles from Thirsk to Yarm. He must have made extremely early starts, because he would arrive at the Yarm shop at 9am.

Twenty minutes a mile is normally considered a respectable achievement, but Thomas, who by this time was a Methodist local preacher, well used to covering long distances to outlying chapels, would probably have managed 15 minutes to the mile

Even at this rate, however, he would have had to depart from Thirsk at 4am!

He continued to run the Yarm business for some years before closing it down to concentrate on Thirsk.

Thomas married Elizabeth Dale in 1834, a woman puritanically strict in religious matters, and a stern disciplinarian in the home. Tall, cool, self-reliant and of great determination, she twice put burglars to flight without arousing her husband from his bed.

Elizabeth had been acquainted with Thomas from an early age, having, as a teenager nursed him devotedly throughout his attack of typhus.

She bore him seven children, of whom the eldest, William, Bill's grandfather, was the only one to survive to a respectable age.

It was a marriage afflicted by stark tragedy.

Four of their offspring, Ann, Thomas, Mary and Frances succumbed to tuberculosis, one of the scourges of the age. Another daughter, Elizabeth, who was married to Joseph Hare, of Balk, near Thirsk, produced 11 children, but died in childbirth at the age of 41.

Jackson Foggitt appeared to have established himself as a farmer in Sowerby, Thirsk, but subsequently went to the USA, although the reason for this is not known. Born in 1832, he too passed away at an early age in 1865, although whether of tuberculosis is also unknown.

Elizabeth herself fell victim to the disease in 1861, aged 55, and along with her husband is buried in Sowerby churchyard. Thomas died in 1885, aged 75.

Their eldest son, having been sent away to school in Tadcaster at the age of ten, managed to escape tuberculosis possibly because he was prevented from coming into contact with other members of the family, and in due course it fell to him to redress the tragedies which had befallen the others.

He married Elizabeth Blackett, daughter of a Thirsk currier (leather worker) in 1857, and they became the proud parents of 12 children, who with their father will feature in a later chapter, since all of them are remembered by Bill — some more vividly than others.

Finally William, the youngest son of Thomas and Ann Foggitt, succeeded to his brother's shop in Yarm, but later moved to Darlington, where he ran his own pharmacy business in High Row for many years.

He was involved in the formation of the local branch of the Onward Building Society, and was elected to Darlington council, eventually becoming mayor.

CHAPTER 2

BURIED IN THIRSK - THE WOMAN WHO "WENT DOWN" WITH THE TITANIC

If you were trying to create a country character, especially one with the gift of being able to consult nature on what the weather had in store, you could do worse than give him a name like Foggitt.

Rich in texture, it has a ring of rustic authority about it, and suggests a long line of ancestors. The name positively reeks of quirkiness, and wisdom handed down from generation to generation. It incorporates a hint of roast chestnuts and home made wine, and has a quality that makes people feel comfortable.

This simple analysis sums up Bill Foggitt, weatherman extraordinary, of Thirsk, North Yorkshire, more accurately than a snapshot.

Behind him, stretching back to the 1480's, if one accepts the argument advanced by Dr Paul Foggitt, lie generations of Foggetts, Fogards, Foggards and Foogotts, originating in the north east.

On the other hand, if one is to believe the tale handed down by Bill's great-grandfather, Thomas Jackson Foggitt, the family, consisting of ardent Protestants, emigrated to this country in the 1500s to escape the wrath of the Pope, and became alum workers in Cleveland.

Whatever the case, it was Thomas Jackson whose love of nature and knowledge of pharmacy gave rise to a flowering of these interests in succeeding generations, and created a business which once rivalled Boots', the Chemists.

Thomas was born in the Blue Bell Inn at Egglescliffe, looking out across the wide River Tees to Yarm, then part of North Yorkshire, This was somewhat ironical, because he was to become a powerful and much-loved Wesleyan preacher in the days when the Methodist ministry was actively castigating the evils of drink. He would think nothing of walking to remote Chapels to preach, taking a crust with friends on the way.

However, his parents were devout people, and there is no evidence to suggest that, even if alcohol was served, it was in any other than a detached way of earning a living.

It is a safe assumption that drunks and roisterers got short thrift. Indeed, the Foggitts may have attracted a lot of trade to their coaching inn by providing hot beverages and food to travellers and stagecoach drivers.

While at school, Thomas became fascinated by accounts of the disastrous flooding at Yarm in 1771, which devastated the town, killing more than 50 people.

As a mighty wall of water rolled down Teesdale from the river's source on Cross Fell (2,930 feet), the highest point on the Pennines, there was no way of warning the town, and there was no time for many people to escape before the flood burst into Yarm.

Thomas was able to see high water mark indicators in the town, and wondered whether similar catastrophes could be avoided through advance knowledge.

The only way of accomplishing this, he reasoned, would be by noting at what times of the year climactic extremes occurred, and the nature of weather conditions leading up to them.

Freak weather in the mountains to the west, such as cloudbursts or sudden thaws, causing masses of snow to melt precipitately, could turn the Tees into a roaring giant.

High Force, where the river hurls itself over 60 feet high cliffs, gives a good indication of the speed and power of floodwater, turning the gorge below into a cauldron of such savagery that the onlooker can hardly believe his eyes.

Before the days of telephones and motor vehicles, the only way of warning villages and towns like Yarm would have been by teams of galloping horsemen, and these would have been almost impossible to muster at short notice.

And so, in 1830, Thomas began his great recording project, which included wind directions and temperatures. And as his facts and figures accumulated, he began to observe that the weather followed a pattern of cycles.

Since he left Yarm in 1836, however, it is not known whether a somewhat crude early warning system, based on weather cycles, was ever put into operation.

Thomas jotted most of his findings down on pieces of paper, several of which survive to this day. He was also an excellent writer, and gave graphic descriptions of outstanding meteorological events, such as his account of a startling display of aurora borealis (northern lights) in October 1870.

He marvelled, "It was a magnificent coloured curtain of light in the eastern sky beyond the Hambleton Hills. Many people in and around Thirsk came out of their homes, some clad in their night attire, to gaze in awe, imagining they were witnessing the reflection of some mighty conflagration."

The Franco-Prussian war was raging at the time, and many onlookers thought that the fires from the continent were being reflected by the clouds.

Thomas also recorded the most ferocious gale of the 19th century. It occurred on December 28th, 1879, and was so violent that it caused the collapse of the Tay Bridge, connecting Edinburgh and Dundee across the estuary of the River Tay, at a point where it is about one and a half miles wide.

The bridge, which had been opened only six months before, was built of wrought iron, instead of the newly-introduced Bessemer steel, which was thought to be unsafe. It was so buffeted by the tempest that its central girders were hurled into the water, 160 feet below.

A train crossing at the time also toppled into the estuary, killing 80 men, women and children. It was a disaster which stunned the nation.

As a result, however, the Forth railway bridge which was built later of steel, was so strong that engineers say it could never suffer a similar fate.

Not only did Thomas record this tragedy, he also told an eerie story in connection with it.

It happened on the same evening as the disaster, while a service was taking place in Thirsk Methodist chapel.

All at once, in the middle of his address, the minister went deathly pale and gasped out to his congregation, "Friends, I can't go on. I have just seen something terrible happening."

With that, he uttered a hasty benediction, and hurried from the chapel, leaving bewildered worshippers looking at each other, and wondering what mysterious insight the minister had experienced.

The time was established later as exactly that of the train plunging into the water. Thomas afterwards informed his family that the minister had told him he had seen a vision of a train falling from a bridge - yet it was not until the following Tuesday that news of the catastrophe reached Thirsk.

In an age when science has taken a good deal of mystique from the para-normal, it is nevertheless difficult to explain how a minister, cocooned in his pulpit, and observed by the congregation, could have "seen" what was happening.

Yet many people have described seeing through "windows" in the dimensionary curtain, and this was obviously a vivid case of extra sensory perception.

Thomas also used to relate the background to the Foggitt family, and over the years the tale has been repeated so often that it has become accepted fact - to all except Dr Foggitt.

Surprisingly, Thomas revealed that the Foggitts came from southern Italy, and on settling in the Cleveland area, where they found work in the alum industry, were known by local people as Foggia-ites after the town from which they hailed.

This was such a tongue-twister, however, that the name was rapidly shortened to Foggitts.

The story made for a charming piece of family history, but on reading Harry Mead's fascinating book, "Inside the North York Moors", one is tempted to wonder whether a little embroidery might be added.

The book tells us that England's first alum mine was established at Belman Bank, Guisborough, the ancient capital of Cleveland, in 1595. It is believed to have commenced operations after the squire of Guisborough, Sir Thomas Chaloner, while on a trip to the continent, noticed similar colouring between leaves near the pope's alum mines, and those on Belman Bank.

A frost-resistant clay, mostly white, but with yellow and blue speckles, was also common to both districts.

In the buccaneering style of the times, Sir Thomas is reputed to have bribed some of the Pope's workers to leave Italy, and to have smuggled them out of the country in casks, for which he incurred a papal curse.

Now a papal curse is not to be sneezed at. Its message is all-embracing, to say the least, and opens by beseeching: "By the authority of God Almighty, the Father, Son and Holy Ghost, and of the undefiled Virgin Mary, mother and patroness of our Saviour, and of all the celestial virtues, angels, archangels, thrones, dominions, powers, cherubins and seraphins, and of the holy patriarchs, prophets and of all the apostles and evangelists, and of the holy innocents, who in the sight of the Holy Lamb are found worthy to sing the new song of the holy martyrs and holy confessors, and of the holy virgins, and of all the saints, together with the holy and elect of God, May he be damned."

Quite a galaxy to be ranged against Sir Thomas, and the curse left no stone unturned as far as his daily life was concerned.

'May he be damned wherever he be, whether in the house or the stables, the garden or the field, or the highway, or in the path or in the wood, or in the water, or in the church.

"May he be cursed in living, in dying, eating or drinking, in being hungry, in being thirsty.

"May he be cursed in sleeping, in slumbering, in walking, in standing, in sitting, in lying, in working, in resting, in pissing, in shitting and in blood letting.

"May he be cursed in all the faculties of his body.

"May he be cursed inwardly and outwardly. May he be cursed in the hair of his head. May he be cursed in his brains and in his vertex, in his temple, in his forehead, in his ears, in his eyebrows, in his cheeks, in his jaw bones, in his nostrils, in his foreteeth and grinders, in his lips, in his throat, in his shoulders, in his wrists, in his arms in his hands, in his fingers."

The Pope was obviously taking no chance on Sir Thomas eluding the net! However, I have no record of whether the curse caught him up, although it certainly gave witchdoctors something to live up to.

Whatever the truth about the Foggitt beginnings, when Bill peers into his shaving mirror, he sees a fair, ruddy complexion, quite different from that of his supposed Italian ancestors.

Bill's grandfather, William Foggitt, was born in 1835. He remembers him only as a stern figure with a handsome white beard before he died in 1917 when Bill was only four.

However, there remains ample testimony to William's standing in the community, and in national botanical circles.

While at school he collected no fewer than 500 specimens of British plants, which he pressed and catalogued - an auspicious start to his botanical pursuits.

Leaving school at 13, while apprenticed in his father's business, he became friendly with John Gilbert Baker, a youth of similar tastes. Over the years their joint rambles, often covering many miles under sometimes trying conditions, resulted in a fine herbarium, and they co-operated in founding the first Natural History Society in Thirsk, in 1853.

The pair remained firm friends after Baker, who lived in Baker's Alley, Thirsk, where a plaque is dedicated to him, achieved fame by being appointed curator of the Royal Kew Herbarium in London.

They were undoubtedly among the leading botanical scientists of their day, and both became Fellows of the Linnaean Society, the famous botanical group founded in London in 1788 in honour of the great Swedish botanist, Carl Linnaeus.

William was well-respected in Thirsk as a JP, as well as a prominent businessman.

He showed the same interest as his father in meteorological matters, and eagerly perpetuated the family records after the latter's death, if anything chronicling events on a more scientific basis.

Bill told me a little known story about the day his grandfather, who, presumably with Gilbert Baker, was arrested as a spy by the Austrian police before the start of the first world war.

"Apparently the pair were in a clump of bushes where they had spotted an interesting specimen, when they were arrested by the police as acting suspiciously. The story goes that they spent an uncomfortable night in the cells, but in the morning their credentials were checked, and they were released with profuse apologies." In these cynical times a different construction would doubless be put on this story!

There is also a story, which if true, reveals a darker side to William's personality. It seems he had a lady friend in Northallerton, whom he used to entertain in an upper room at the town's Station Hotel.

It was said that a group of station porters put a ladder up to an upstairs window to verify the story, although what they saw is unrecorded.

The story may be apocryphal, but Bill distinctly remembers his outspoken Aunt Kate telling him how she tried several times to get her father away from "that Mrs C ..."

William's eldest son, Thomas Jackson Foggitt, born in 1858, although not elected to the Linnaean Society, was equally famous as a botanist, once informing young Bill that he had a specimen of every plant in Great Britain. He had a consuming interest in botany, and was a member of several societies. His kindness to other botanists was unfailing.

He travelled all over the British Isles, and even visited Switzerland in the search for plants and wild flowers. He would visit places such as the Channel Islands, Devon and Cornwall, often looking for a single specimen, and was especially fond of Scotland, where he was once lost in mist among precipices, and on another occasion sat up all night on a broken chair in a crofter's cottage.

Thomas, too, ranked with the greatest botanists of the time. And his zeal in continuing to record weather statistics was no less than that of his father. He started supplying rainfall figures to the Meteorological Office around 1914, and kept these up until he died in 1934, at which point Bill's father took over, until his own death in 1962.

The Met Office recognised 75 years service by the Foggitt family in 1989, when Bill received a handsome book about the British countryside.

An unsmiling Uncle Tom still looks down sombrely from the living room wall of South Villa - the only photograph to grace it.

For most of his life, Thomas lived at Stoneybrough House, a large detached dwelling in its own grounds, about half a mile from South Villa. He remained single for many years, eventually marrying his father's housekeeper, Fanny Sophia Body, in 1919.

Apparently his liaison with Fanny incurred her father's disapproval, but she proved to be a devoted wife, and was very popular among the family. Tragically she died six years later, in 1925, and Thomas remarried in 1929.

His second wife, Gertrude Bacon, was a formidable personality, and a pioneer in female aviation, becoming one of the country's first woman balloonists. She wrote a book entitled "Memories of Land and Sky", and shared her husband's love of botany and natural history.

After his death at the age of 76, Gertrude moved to Hampshire, where she died in 1949.

There were no children of this, or Thomas's first marriage. Gertrude was not approved of by members of the Foggitt family, who thought she was covetous of his money, because his estate of £9.000 was much less than they had expected.

Bill said he remembered Uncle Tom with admiration, tempered by reservation. "A Justice of the Peace, he travelled everywhere by chauffeur-driven car; a stern man who created something of a stir by marrying his father's housekeeper.

"He used to take my brother and me on some of his plant-gathering expeditions, and I particularly remember travelling to Richmond, North Yorkshire, where he knew of the existence of a rare species of willow.

"He was trying to reach out for a cutting, and told me to hold on to a rather whippy branch to steady him. Unfortunately my hand slipped; the branch snapped back, and Uncle Tom became temporarily airborne.

"In retrospect I found this extremely comical, because I doubt whether anyone had ever seen His Worship in such an undignified situation, frantically grabbing at the nearest branch for support, but at the time I was distinctively apprehensive.

"After all, here was a man who had sentenced a harmless drunk to hard labour, apparently just for being high-spirited in the street.

"However, although the anticipated wigging was not forthcoming, he fixed me with a look which spoke volumes."

Added Bill, "Uncle Tom could be very rude. I once offered to measure the rainfall for him, only to be told he would rather see blood spilt than water!

"I have often wondered what this stern-minded man would say if he were here now, in the knowledge that his once beautiful house had been flattened to make way for new dwellings."

Bill still has a collection of about 100 plants, collected while out with his uncle.

Bill's other uncles and aunts, in order of birth, were William Crossley, of whom little is known, except that he married the daughter of a farmer in the Aberdeen area.

Both died in the Southport of Ormskirk area of Lancashire at the age of 35.

John Blackett ran three chemist's shops in Southport, where he was leader of the town council for six years, and was elected to the aldermanic bench. He also became a keen botanist, which he combined with ornithology. He and his wife had five children.

He left Southport around 1920, and set up a business in Kirby Lonsdale, where he died in 1942, aged 80.

Mary Frances Elizabeth married Samuel Ingham, a Thirsk draper. There were no children. They married in 1885, and Bill tells an amusing story about his Aunt Frances (she insisted on being called Awnt Frawnces) returning home the following day, tearfully telling her mother that her husband had "tried to do naughty things to me in bed."

However, according to the 1891 census, Frances and Samuel were living together above the shop in the market place, so the once staid and inexperienced young lady presumably found that naughty could also be nice!

Auntie Ada lived at home until she was at least 26. In 1892 she married Robert Tennant, a bank employee, who eventually became manager of the bank in Thirsk. They had three daughters.

Gilbert Baker did not live up to his illustrious name. He attended Wharfedale College, Boston Spa, until he was 13, but doesn't appear anywhere in the British Isles according to the 1891 census, and it is believed he may have been sent abroad after causing some sort of family offence. He is thought to have gone to America, and to have died there.

Frederick Addison seems to have been of a similar bent, causing offence to the family, and being "banished" to South Africa, where he died in 1927.

Eleanor Jane sustained severe burns and died at the tender age of 16 after her clothing caught fire. The year was 1887.

Ernest Alfred died at the age of 22 in 1895, after collapsing while playing football.

Catherine Isabella - Bill's favourite aunt, who was outspoken and very popular with younger members of the Foggitt family - married Herbert Mawer quite late in life.

Said Bill, "She certainly believed in calling a spade a spade. After a boring address by a Methodist minister, she told him to his face that he was a 'rambling old bugger', which of course, in those days was a monumental affront to the cloth, and only someone like Aunt Kate could have got away with it.

"She had a male friend for many years, and after he died, she got married to a man with the same surname. At the wedding she was heard to whisper to a friend, 'Right name, wrong man.' Still, I suppose even Aunt Kate couldn't be blamed for wanting companionship late in life.

"When I was working in Birmingham, and not earning much money, she one turned to me and said, 'Now Billy, you won't mind me asking, but are you all right for money? I told her I was, which wasn't entirely true, but I suspect she knew, anyway.

"Aunt Kate never had much money herself, but she left me £49 when she died, and that, to me, was quite a considerable sum."

And now we come to Louisa, the most interesting member of the family - if the most notorious.

She is the aunt who "went down with the Titanic" - but is buried in Thirsk Cemetery.

Her story illustrates some of the attitudes of behaviour, which nowadays would hardly cause an eyebrow to be raised. It is a bizarre and tragic story, that has its roots in family pride and social pretensions.

Born in 1876, she married William Wellbank Hall, son of the landlord of Thirsk's Golden Fleece Hotel, in 1899, at the age of 23. Her husband was 41 at the time, and took over the hotel on his father's death.

In 1912, Louisa fell for the charms of a flashy racegoer, who was presumably staying at the Golden Fleece during the Thirsk race meeting. Something very intense must have happened between them, because she suddenly left the hotel, her husband and three children, to go off to London with him.

However, as so often happens with flashy types, her paramour soon tired of her, and poor Louisa, too proud, too scared, or too ashamed to return home, was forced to seek employment as a skivvy, working in the kitchens of a London hotel.

She became so poor that she had to pawn her wedding ring to obtain some money.

Her departure hit the families like a bombshell. Their solid, middle class standing was shaken to the foundations by the scandal, and a way had to be found to explain Louisa's disappearance.

Whoever came up with it, the answer proved simple. It was 1912, the year the Titanic went down, so the story was put about that she had gone down with the ill-fated liner, and it appears her children were somehow led to believe that this was a fact.

In fact, her son, William Hall, who eventually settled in Australia, still believed this fabrication when he was interviewed there in 1993, and not only that - he had apparently convinced himself that he, too, was on the Titanic!

A daughter, Violet, married and for a time lived in Rio de Janeiro, before returning to live in London. She died in 1981.

Another daughter, Margaret, married a General Halliday, and is thought to have a son, Cyril Sebriat Halliday. She settled in Malta, but little is known of her.

Louisa continued working in the hotel kitchen, and Dr Foggitt, who has carefully researched the whole affair, said, "It seems that she ate some shellfish which had been left over from a dinner, and as a consequence developed typhoid fever. She was admitted to the London Fever Hospital in Liverpool Road, and died there on October 26th, 1916 at the age of 40.

"The family were informed of her impending death, and her sister, Annie Ada Tennant, went to London; redeemed the wedding ring, and arranged for her body to be returned to Thirsk, where she was buried in the local cemetery. The headstone records her death as being in 1918, but a mistake was obviously made, because I have Louisa's death certificate in my possession."

Of William Hall, Dr Foggitt said, "Little is known of him, except that he obviously believed the story of the Titanic to be true, and had convinced himself that he was on board at the time." He added, "I find it astonishing, if the truth was kept from Louisa's children."

In May 1993, Dr Foggitt received an unexpected telephone call from Australia, from a Mr Ian Griggs, who said he was interested in the story that Louisa had gone down with the Titanic.

He had been interviewing William Hall, with a view to recounting the story as told by him.

Subsequently, after being informed that the story was simply not true, Mr Griggs wrote to Dr Foggitt saying he had carried out research ever since he had met William, when he was 92.

He went on, "Of course the Titanic legend reared its head with imagination, fired by over 30 years of reading and refinement. In fact when he (William) visited Thirsk in 1970, I am surprised that he was not informed of the truth then, especially considering his mother's grave is right there.

"Unfortunately the publication of his memoirs, in which the Titanic episode would have featured prominently, has come to a grinding halt."

Mr Griggs added that one thing which was most disappointing was William's alleged memory of the tune which he heard being played by the Titanic's bank as she went down. "This has been a source of great confusion for decades. William has casually remarked that he heard 'Autumn' by Cecil Chaminade. The extraordinary fact now remains that this could possibly have been the very tune played, because it was contemporary and well-known, and would have suited the event."

Dr Foggitt replied, enclosing a copy of the Foggitt family history, which he hoped might be of use to Mr Griggs. He said, "The elopement to London with a total stranger was obviously a severe affront to the family, and it is fairly clear that attempts to cover up this murky episode were made - pretty effectively, since the story of the loss on the Titanic was apparently believed to be true."

He added, "I see that William is supposed to have gone to school at Archbishop Holgate's and St.. Peter's schools in York, and as there is no record of his enrolment at St.. Peter's, one cannot help wondering if this may also be a questionable episode in his life."

Nowadays, of course, the story about Louisa going down on the Titanic, and the subsequent brainwashing of her children reads like a fairy-tale, but in those days wives who scandalised prominent families in the way she did, had little redress or rights, particularly when it came to deserting her children. One can well imagine Louisa being ordered never to darken the family doorstep again and forbidden even to communicate with her children, while her compliance would be virtually guaranteed by her sense of sheer shame. Poor Louisa would, in fact, probably have ceased to exist.

However, it is somewhat comforting to know that her sister, Ada, was at the hospital when she died, and arranged for her to be buried in her mother's grave in Thirsk. This was in 1916, and her father would have been interred in the same grave a year later.

The headstone was probably erected later, and a mistake was probably made by the stone-mason when recording Louisa's death in 1918.

Bill has little knowledge of the scandal or the Titanic tale. He said, "William used to come over the Thirsk brash, brown and athletic looking for his age, and stay with a cousin, but he never said anything to me about the Titanic or Aunt Louisa".

And so we come to the youngest of William's family, Bill's father, Benjamin Foggitt.

Quite a lot will be said about him in the following chapter, but suffice it to say here that he continued the tradition laid down by his grandfather, and followed by his father and eldest brother, of dedication to the family pharmacy business; custodianship of the records, and to the natural world, in his case the study of ornithology and entomology, in which he also achieved distinction.

Born in 1881, Benjamin married Elizabeth Bradley in 1912, and in 1921, while his grandfather was still alive, moved into South Villa with their three children, Bill, born 1913, Benjamin, born 1916 and Elizabeth, born 1918.

He trained as a pharmacist, and joined the family business, later becoming a partner of Thomas, until his brother died in 1934.

He too, became a prominent businessman, as well as being active in the Methodist church, but in 1935 Foggitt's shop was taken over by Boots, and a famous name disappeared, along with 100 years of tradition.

Benjamin, ironically enough, enjoyed shooting as a hobby, and somehow reconciled this with his ardent study of birds. He had a dislike of doctors, although a local GP was often with him on shoots, and apparently, even when dying in Thirsk market place, where he collapsed in 1962, refused medical attention.

An appraisal of his father is taken up by Bill, who was to become the most famous member of the Foggitts in terms of media recognition.

CHAPTER 3

A MAN OF GOD - AND THE GUN

I say he became famous in terms of media recognition, because although Bill has compiled his own records for the past 32 years, and listed his own observations and interpretations of the natural world, he is the first to admit that he has drawn on the knowledge, archives and family sayings when asked for pronouncements on the weather.

However, this is not to detract from his own achievements, which have caught the attention of newspapers and television since 1966, and rightly propelled him to the fore of the country's amateur meteorologists.

Now 86, Bill lives a frugal life on the outskirts of Thirsk, actually within the boundary of the parish of Bagby.

His only companions are his neighbour and housekeeper, Mrs Betty Cook, a retired nurse who is devoted to his welfare, and, as you would expect, plenty of visitors.

He has a cheerful nature, and his blue eyes, which give no indication of his failing sight, have a ready twinkle, despite the many squalls in his life, some of which have threatened to capsize him.

His sense of humour is infectious, and his friends know him as an excellent mimic, which once earned him great popularity in army concerts for his impersonations of people like Churchill ("We will fight them on the beaches ...") and Neville Chamberlain ("I have here a piece of paper ...").

Specialists have told him they can do nothing about his eyes, so now, when he sallies forth each morning for a pint of beer, and to do his shopping, he has to make his way along busy main roads, nearly half a mile into Thirsk, with the help of a white stick, which he waves indignantly at vehicles passing too closely, or at what he considers to be excessive speed.

For Bill can never forget the accident, in 1966, near his home, which nearly cost him his right leg. An additional hazard is his defective hearing, although this was improved by the acquisition of a hearing aid.

He has a great liking for his home town, and especially the company of his friends, whom he refers to as his "magic circle", but is always glad to get home, although sadly, he knows he will no longer be given a rapturous welcome by his little dog Polly who died last year. "Always a welcome," he used to chuckle, as his pet almost dragged him into the sitting room by his stick.

When Polly was younger he caused a mild stir by protecting her from male canines with a pair of women's tights, suitably cut in the right places. "It may have looked funny, but it was a practical way of dealing with the matter," he declared.

Betty prepares two meals a day for him, because the kitchen is now virtually unusable, and Bill augments these with a diet of six bananas. The table dwarfs him, and when he looks round at the empty spaces, he sometimes thinks of those animated family debates about nature which took place round it.

"The weather was a hotly-debated subject with us. We would discuss cloud formations, wind direction, sunsets and other indicators, before giving our opinions on what sort of weather conditions would follow.

"We weren't expected to get it wrong, otherwise searching questions were asked."

Bill has a countryman's mistrust of mechanical devices. He knows nothing about the stock exchange, nor about the wiles of human nature. He has never really got over being locked in a Birmingham public lavatory for two hours, until his cries for help were answered.

Slick patter has as much penetration as raindrops on his trusty umbrella. He simply doesn't understand it.

He is a complete stranger to hypocrisy, intrigue or subterfuge.

For the gentle weatherman really is that rare creature these days - an innocent abroad. His naivete has got him involved in several tricky situations, but, almost as if fate were ashamed at taking advantage of such a guileless human being, he has always come through virtually unscathed.

These are the qualities that endear him to people. They regard him as a character because of his stubborn adherence to an old-fashioned way of life, which these days is seen as eccentricity; his homespun theories; the mishaps which constantly lie in wait for him, and his self-effacing humour.

They are also protective of him. Shopkeepers, hoteliers, supermarket or bank staff can't do enough for him. They will steer him in the right direction, explain how much he's spent, and how much change he has. At the Chemists the staff even used to change his razor blades for him.

Whereas Thirsk people looked up to James Herriot (Alf Wight) as a "lovely man" and protected his much-loved privacy, they probably have an even greater affection for Bill, because of his vulnerability, accessibility, or simply because he is "one of them".

As a Methodist local preacher for more than 60 years, he sees the hand of God in human and natural law. For him the instincts of plants and animals are, within their own kingdom, equally as efficacious as anything technology can produce.

He likes nothing better than to reminisce with his "magic circle", who are always genuinely interested in his theories and stories, and one of them, a retired headmaster and eminent educationalist, has taught him things about nature that even he was not aware of.

For although newspaper headlines such as "Foggitt's Lore", "Foggitt's Forecast", "Fair Stands The Spring For Foggitt", and that sub-editor's classic, "Vane Predictions Of A Humble Man" have testified to his expertise, Bill is always ready to listen to others, and, if necessary, add their folklore to his own vast knowledge.

For instance, he always believed that if rooks built their nests high, it presaged a fine summer with little wind, but when a south of England countryman told him that rooks often repaired their existing nests, he began to wonder if his theory was open to doubt.

South Villas, built in 1830, once stood amidst acres of green fields in which wildlife abounded, and in which, as a young boy, his knowledge of natural history took root.

Nowadays his home is surrounded by commercial and industrial units on a council-owned site, for the establishment of which he was obliged to sell several acres in order to keep a roof over his head.

The estate is kept at arm's length by walls, bushes and trees which camouflage South Villa to some extent, and form an oasis for what wildlife is left.

Despite its peeling sage-green paint, the old house retains an aura of dignity, rather as an elderly lady who has known better days, stoutly maintains her pride by wearing her widow's "weeds".

Bill has insufficient money to have it restored to its former grandeur, but the house is sturdy and sound.

He says of his housekeeper, who nowadays monitors the rainfall, barometer and temperature readings, and keeps in touch with the Met-Office, "Betty has looked after Mother and me for more than 30 years, and frankly, since Mother died in 1977 at the age of 96, I don't know what I would have done without her. If it weren't for her I would probably have to go into a home, and that would be heartbreaking for me.

"She often tells me off, but as I am a very forgetful person, I suppose it is deserved. At any rate, I am deeply grateful for what she does."

South Villa has a well-kept lawn, but the pond which gave Bill his information about frog spawn, has now dried up and become overgrown, and he cannot afford the luxury of a gardener to rehabilitate it.

Apart from his bedroom and huge bathroom, he confines himself to a high-ceilinged sitting room with a spacious bay window, which is dominated by a massive Victorian sideboard and a mahogany, glass-fronted bookcase in which he keeps his books and records.

Many of the books are about botany and religion.

A chenille-covered table of majestic proportions, and a couple of high-backed chairs complete the intimidating scene, while a few well-worn armchairs and a modest fireplace provide Bill's only comforts.

His personal diaries, dating back to 1927, occupy a small bookcase next to the fireplace. Many of them are dog-eared; a few are missing, but the rest are full of information about Bill's life since he started keeping them. Dr. Foggitt has now painstakingly transferred their contents onto his computer - just in case.

As he climbed the wide stairway to show me round, he casually tore off a piece of wallpaper which was hanging free. "Can't have the place looking untidy," he muttered. He is fond of telling people the house is haunted, but admits he has never seen anything untoward. "An aunt once assured me, however, that she had seen a hand opening the bookcase door, and I assume it belonged to grandfather William. Mind you, some of my aunts were a funny lot.

"Aunt Frances was the one who ran home to mother after her wedding night. She was full of airs and graces, and once told my sister Betty to call her Awnt Frawnces - not Auntie Frances. On another occasion we were attending a funeral service, and Awnt Frawnces remarked with some asperity, "I do think Betty should be wearing black!

"Betty would be just about five at the time!

"Some of the family thought they were rather grand because they had a family pew in the chapel, but their haughtiness came unstuck once.

"As a service was about to begin, a lady with a stick attempted to enter it. 'You can't come in here,' trilled the aunts, 'this is a rented pew.'

The lady apologised, explaining that she was the wife of the new minister. "Oh, that's all right then,' replied my aunts, rather shamefacedly. "You'd better come in."

"Aunt Kate, however, was much more friendly and down-to-earth. She would walk miles into the countryside just to see people 'buried with ham' (a reference to the traditional ham teas that followed a funeral) whether or not she knew the deceased. This gatecrashing didn't exactly endear her to relatives, but I thought the world of her."

Bill remembers his father with mixed feelings, sometimes verging on resentment, but more often than not, with gratitude.

Benjamin Foggitt had all the qualities which had elevated his grandfather, father, and eldest brother. Dedicated to Methodism and business; intolerant of breaches of protocol, and a pillar of the community, he represented a now almost forgotten era when Britain controlled a quarter of the globe, and the principles of duty, diligence and dignity were paramount.

In those days children rarely answered back, and the authority of policemen, businessmen, teachers, town councillors and the clergy was hardly ever challenged.

This chemist's shop in Thirsk market place was booming, as indeed was Thirsk itself. In medical matters it played a much more important part than pharmacists do today, even extending its services to the veterinary profession.

At one time the wholesale department of Foggitts, situated in the former Thirsk drill hall, now R S Hall, Engineering, claimed to be as influential as Boots.

Bill, who served a four-year apprenticeship in the shop, remembers the premises as being gloomy, with gas lamps and very basic outside lavatories.

Herbal remedies were highly thought of, and the various herbs, each with their Latin names, were kept in separate drawers behind the counter. Bill was expected to know them all.

Today, there is a renewal of faith in the efficacy of herbal palliatives, but one seldom hears of other aids offered by Foggitt's and other chemists before the second world war: Carters Little Liver Pills; Fenning's Fever Cure; Scott's Emulsion; Friar's Balsam; Cascara; Phyllosan (fortifies the over-forties"), or Malt Extract, to name just a few.

Looming over the multiplicity of drawers, cupboards, tins, brightly-coloured bottles or packets, were huge carboys, filled with coloured liquids, proclaiming the pharmacist's trade.

But Bill was never happy in the shop, and left after four years to become a chemist's assistant in Bridlington, subsequently moving in the same capacity to Biggleswade. He said, "It was a rather dreary, humdrum existence in Thirsk. I had to be there by 9 am and was often still behind the counter at 7 pm. Not being qualified, I was unable to make up prescriptions, and was confined to selling goods in packets, bottles or tins. We also sold cigarettes and tobacco in those days.

"It was such a monotonous job, that I took, almost as a form of escape, a course in the scientific development of the mind and memory with the Pelman Institute. I completed the course to the satisfaction of the directors, but despite this, failed my pharmaceutical examination, much to my father's disgust. I enjoyed the course, and felt a wiser person at the end of it, but it was no good - I just couldn't come to terms with science, no matter how hard I tried." An entry in his diary for 1932 records his weighing out, or mixing, such exotic substances as hellebore powder, Epsom salts, cattle salts, senna leaves and pods, erica nut powder, bicarbonate of soda, tartaric acid, "Felon" drinks, sulphur, borax and Glauber's salts.

He also carried out certain administrative tasks such as writing out cheques and sending off letters.

Was it because of the pressure of the job, or simply curiosity, when he wrote in his diary on March 12th, 1932 "Commenced smoking my pipe this evening?"

Whatever it was, Bill recalled "I didn't smoke it for long, preferring cigarettes, of which I smoked about ten a day until my accident in 1966, when I stopped completely. I must say, it doesn't seem to have done me any harm, having got to the age of 86."

Townspeople accorded Mr Foggitt Senior almost obsequious respect as a dispenser of medical wisdom, who always listened gravely while they described their various ailments, such as sore throats, head colds, coughs, asthma, creaking backs or muscular pains, before prescribing what he assured them would bring relief.

He obviously had the greatest faith in his own remedies, because he hardly ever saw a doctor until he was old and suffered heart attacks.

The shop unfailingly opened at 8 am, and didn't close until 7 pm. On Saturdays business went on until 10 pm.

Those were golden years in Thirsk, now a ghost town by comparison. Unassailed by competition from supermarkets, and surrounded by a reservoir of agriculture (which it still is), the town was a mini-metropolis of business activity.

Stalls covered most of the cobbled market place, with stallholders' strident cries echoing from rustic brick buildings, and every yard and alley was home to a variety of enterprises, including cobblers, potters, carpenters, blacksmiths, tinsmiths or saddlers.

Butchers would carry on a roaring trade, travelling round the pubs with their baskets of bargain-priced cuts. Countrywomen came into the town on charabancs, and farmers' wives would offer eggs, bacon, cheese and livestock for sale.

It was among this bedlam of activity that young Bill, on his way home from the local grammar school, was accosted by a cheerful stallholder, based outside his father's shop, and recalled with a grimace, "He was selling hair restorer, and seemed to be making great play out of the fact that he was opposite our shop. 'Now then, young fella,' he shouted (I can never see why he was addressing me), 'here's the real thing. Grow hair on an egg it will. Now that old bugger (pointing at the shop) reckons to be selling the same sort of thing, so why's he as bald as a badger, eh?'"

Bill continued, "He was coarse, and I didn't like to hear my father spoken about in that way, but in his rather crude way, I suppose he had a point. Father didn't have a lot of hair, and if he *was* selling hair restorer I don't suppose it would have done much good. But then neither would the stuff the market man was selling, either."

Mr Foggitt never missed a chapel service, and invariably took his family with him. Said Bill, "For worship and funerals, whatever the weather, he always wore a black overcoat, bowler hat, shiny shoes and spats, and carried a rolled umbrella.

"He never missed a funeral, whatever the denomination of the deceased. So many people had gone to him for prescriptions that he felt it was his bounden duty to pay his respects when they passed on.

"He would tell us to listen to the 'death bell' at the parish church, for instance, and count the number of chimes - 12 for a man; nine for a woman and six for a child.

"If father was not sure whether or not someone had died, he had his own way of finding out.

"He would simply march up to the front door, and if it was the husband who answered, say, 'Good morning, Mr S, and how is your good lady today?' To which the bereaved man would reply, 'Oh Mr Foggitt, didn't you know? She passed away yesterday.'

Of course people used to draw their curtains when someone died, but father had to know the day and time of the funeral as well. He would then doff his hat and offer his condolences. I remember being with him on one of the occasions, and being rather embarrassed by father's directness."

In the early years of Bill's life, entertainment was more or less limited to a crackling radio, visiting relatives, events organised by the local chapel, or as a special treat, going to one of the town's two cinemas one a week.

"I'll never forget the first Christmas after we first got the radio. King George was addressing the nation, and one of my aunts squealed, 'Oh listen, he's talking to us!' But what Bill really looked forward to were those Sunday afternoon strolls with his parents, when the whole family would wander along hedgerows and through woods and fields. Between them they would point out all sorts of interesting plants and birds, and mother, who was a tremendous repository of folklore sayings and rhymes, would repeat these to us, and then counsel us to test their accuracy by our own observations.

"I was particularly intrigued by the behaviour of a flower known as the Scarlet Pimpernel, nicknamed the poor man's weather glass because of its habit of closing its petals when rain was on the way. But there were many others, and even in those days I remember wondering whether they would be of use to me in foretelling weather conditions."

As they trooped along, identifying plants, flowers, birds and insects, and learning about their idiosyncrasies, Bill recalls his father singing hymns concerned with nature.

One which stands out in his mind, ran, "By cool Siloam's shady rill, how sweet the lily grows; how sweet the breath beneath the hill, of Sharon's dewy rose."

He went on, "I have seen Siloam's shady rill during a visit to the Holy Land, but it has either changed, or it was the wrong time of the year, because I can only recall it as a rather muddy pool, and totally uninspiring.

"However, it's a lovely hymn, and it would be churlish of me to mock father's obvious sincerity. It conveys God's love through the beauty of nature. There was another one which included the words, 'We read Thee in the flowers, the trees; the freshness of the fragrant breeze.'

"I don't suppose I was particularly impressed at the time. I remember that father had a rather tuneless voice, but looking back, I realise he was a devout man to whom these hymns really meant something.

"In those days people sang spontaneously at the sheer joy of being in the countryside. How often do you hear that sort of thing now? Do you ever hear groups of healthy people in boots, anoraks and with packs on their backs burst into song as they make their way determinedly along moorland tracks?"

He continued, "When we arrived home we had tea, and father would carry on singing hymns while Mother played the piano. I know it sounds awfully dull and cissyish compared with the wide range of exciting leisure activities today, but what we hadn't experienced, we couldn't miss."

There were, however, other trips which Bill and his younger brother did not find so exciting or relaxing, such as when they accompanied their father into town, and became "young soldiers."

"Father had been a sergeant in the army, stationed in Palestine, and he never forgot it. He maintained his military bearing, and in the absence of squaddies to bawl at, obviously saw us as a couple of likely lads. The result was drill sessions as we walked along.

"The pavement took the place of a parade ground. 'Right!' he would boom, 'you're on parade. Heads back, shoulders straight; left, right, left, right ... aaabout turn!

"We wouldn't be out of short trousers at the time, and I found it all a bit ridiculous, but I suppose in his own way, bearing in mind the military age in which we lived, he genuinely thought he was looking after our welfare. Anyway, we thought his behaviour was a bit over the top, although, as far as I know, father never 'went over the top' during the war.

"He didn't even let up at bedtime. As soon as Ben and I were between the sheets, he would bellow, 'Lights out, lights out!' I suppose on some occasions I must have rebelled, because father would often threaten to turn me out of the house, although I don't know how serious he was.

"I actually had a suitcase packed under the bed, ready to depart at short notice. Mind you, heaven knows where I would have fled to. A sympathetic aunt's I suppose."

Despite his father's pious manner where affairs of business and the chapel were concerned, and his love of hymn singing and nature, Bill is sure he was seized by a blood lust when it came to shooting birds and animals.

"He was a dedicated shooting man, and encouraged Ben and me to take up the challenge. Ben responded enthusiastically, but cutting down wild creatures was not for me.

"Maybe Ben took after father, whereas I had more of my mother's gentle genes in me, but I hated what they were doing, and was therefore relegated to carrying the game bag.

"Everything tumbled into it ... hares, rabbits, pheasants, partridges and pigeons. It seemed to me that they shot anything which moved. Once I put a 'dead' rabbit into the gunny sack, but suddenly it came to life. It had only been stunned. 'Hit it on the back of the neck!' roared father, but the poor creature looked at me piteously, as if to say, 'Why have I deserved this?' and I was too squeamish to kill it.

"This may have earned me my father's contempt, but to this day I abhor the idea of killing wild creatures of sport.

"Hares used to scream when the dogs caught up with them. It was an awful sound that still lingers in my mind. It affected my uncle John as well when he joined a shooting expedition - so much so that he never took up a gun again. He went to Southport, where he opened several shops, and presumably never saw another hare, unless there were game shops in that genteel town.

"I felt physically sick on one shoot when I went up to a pheasant, lying in the grass at Helmsley. I thought it looked very tame, but as I got up to it, I saw that its legs had been shot away. The dogs didn't always pick up wounded birds."

Bill admitted, however, that he might have been somewhat hypocritical. "Friends used to ask me if I ate what my father had shot, and I was ashamed to say I did, although not to have done so would have meant going hungry. But in this respect I wasn't much different from these so-called animal's rights protesters."

He was eight years old when he first became a "minister" - conducting funeral services for dead animals.

"I suppose my sympathy for nature's creatures began about that time, and I was very keen to see them buried properly. This applied equally to wild birds found dead in the garden.

"The funerals were solemn affairs, because we all used to be saddened by their passing. The grave would be dug in the back garden, and

35

I would lead a procession round the house, consisting of my brother and sister, Aunt Nellie, a friend, Francis Kirby, our maid, Emily and sometimes the gardener, Mr Mackereth.

"Although she never took part, Mother would supply flowers from her garden. I would read a short passage from the Bible, and we would sing a hymn. The animal or bird would then be buried, along with a short note. Our hens, of which we were all very fond, used to get the VIP treatment.

"I remember one old Rhode Island Red we called Grandma. It was so old it couldn't walk, and Betty, my sister, used to wheel her about in a pram."

Added Bill, "It all sounds so soppy now, but I still believe animals have souls, and often find myself wondering why humans, many of whom reach the depths of depravity, can imagine heaven is reserved exclusively for them."

Looking back, he perceives that these obsequies probably awakened in him an unconscious desire to become a minister of the church, and although he failed to achieve success in this career, either as a Methodist minister or an Anglican vicar, he has been a Methodist local preacher for more than 60 years, and still enters the pulpit.

But to return to Mr Foggitt, senior. Said Bill, "I was deeply grateful to him for the knowledge he imparted, which has been enormously valuable in my weather predictions. Sometimes he seemed unduly harsh, but I recognise now that it was for my own good, although I couldn't see it at the time. This was to come home to me later when I was sent to boarding school, and realised what a sheltered life I had led."

He cast his mind back to a wet and miserable morning on June 29th, 1927, when his father sowed the seeds of Bill's eventual career as a weather forecaster.

"It was about 4 am when he roused us, and announced that we were going to Wensleydale to witness the total eclipse of the sun. Leyburn, he explained, would be the place where we would see it best.
"All I wanted to do was to turn over and get back to sleep. I didn't feel too well, and was thoroughly miserable by the time we reached Leyburn, and climbed up a footpath known locally as The Shawl.

"Some folk believe it was so named because when Mary, Queen of Scots, was escaping from captivity in nearby Bolton Castle, she dropped her shawl on the path, which led to her recapture.

"When we arrived, the dawn chorus was in full voice. Then suddenly a dark shadow - the moon - started to cross the face of the sun. The birds immediately stopped singing. The temperature fell, and the chattering of onlookers abruptly ceased.

"It was as if we were watching the end of the world, it was so eerie. The darkness lasted for about eight minutes from 6 am. Then slowly the veil was drawn away, and the blessed light returned. The birds resumed their singing, and I felt a great sense of relief as life got back to normal."

Before they left Leyburn, Bill's father turned to him and said, "Now Billy, I want you to record what you have just seen, and if you continue to jot down your observations of the weather, you'll get a new diary for Christmas.

So that was how Bill came to start his diaries, a daily chore he fulfilled for more than 70 years.

Sadly, because of his age, he was unable to accept an invitation to Cornwall last August to see his second eclipse of the century.

His father was a keen amateur astronomer, and used to explain his theory about sunspots and their influence on the weather when Bill enquired what he was doing, looking at the sun through a piece of smoked glass. But this will be dealt with in a later chapter.

Like his brother, Thomas, Foggitt senior could be extremely rude if he chose, according to his son.

Such as the time two young women presented themselves on his doorstop before the second world war, and asked him if he would sign a piece of paper, saying "Peace with Hitler".

"Yes," he barked, "just as long as you get Herr Hitler to sign it first."

The severity of his reaction took the females aback, which led to Bill commenting, "While I agreed with father's point, he was a little harsh on the young women, who were probably well-intentioned, if misguided."

He also considered his father a snob. "He lost no opportunity to be seen with people whom he considered mattered. He kept a box of expensive sweets under the counter, which he used to hand out to the great and the good. For the working class there was a tin of humble lozenges.

"And you can imagine the kerfuffle that went on in the shop, the day Princess Mary walked in unexpectedly. I'll never forget that episode. Father was quite beside himself in his desire to be of service. He nearly knocked me over in his haste to welcome her - not that it mattered a jot to the princess.

"Another example of father's rudeness was later in life, when he was confined to bed with heart trouble. Normally he wouldn't have anything to do with doctors, although one of his shooting pals was a local GP.

"Anyway, on this occasion mother had decided he should take medical advice, but the doctor father knew was away at the time, and a younger partner turned up. 'Who are you, and what are you doing here?' demanded father. 'Mrs Foggitt sent for me,' replied the startled medic. 'Well,' snapped father, 'you can just go away again, because I don't want to see you.'"

Posterity doesn't record what the hapless doctor said on his return to the surgery.

An impatience with Bill's shortcomings soured his relations with his autocratic parent. The future weatherman found it impossible to grasp the principles of maths and science - with the exception of botanical science - although he was excellent at English, and later tried his hand at a couple of novels. Because he lacked the logical mind of the mathematician, he failed to pass the former school certificate examination, and was later to fail his pharmaceutical paper, much to his father's disgust.

His son said, "To be fair, father tried to tutor me in maths, and paid for private tuition so that I might pass my pharmaceutical examination, but it was not use - I just wasn't cut out for a career in this field.

"I can well understand how frustrated and angry he was. After all, he could see three generations of pharmacists slipping away, but the way he pilloried me about my lack of knowledge was simply not called for.

"My ordeal was made worse by his constant references to my brother, and how bright he was. I was not a patch on Benjamin, he used to say, and what made it worse was that he didn't care who he said it in front of. I felt humiliated and just wanted to creep away.

"Figures have always baffled me, but I once got 99 per cent in English at Thirsk grammar school. 'Yes,' my father remarked sarcastically, 'you certainly tell a good tale.' He also used to inform me that I would probably live to a good age, but it wouldn't be through overwork.

"In the end he said I would never make a chemist, but I remained with him as an unqualified assistant for four years, before leaving for a similar post in Bridlington, eventually finishing up in Biggleswade, in Bedfordshire."

One of the most striking memories Bill cherishes, was his father's superb collection of stuffed birds. These took up most of his natural history room, where Bill would gaze at their still vivid plumage in open-mouthed admiration.

"Uncle Tom used to boast that he had a specimen of every plant in the United Kingdom," said Bill, "but father, apparently, ran him close in the context of birds' eggs, although this would be greeted with horror these days."

To Foggitt senior, however, they were ornithological specimens which made an important contribution to natural history studies.

Now only a heron, kingfisher and waterhen are left - shadows of the past in the gloomy recesses of South Villa.

Bill believes his mother, who must have had a touch of steel in her make up, persuaded his father to donate the collections to a museum. "She used to say they were unhealthy things to have about the house, and eventually father gave in and got rid of them, but to me at least, it was a great loss when they went."

Bill began his education at a local school, run by the two daughters of a Methodist minister, before moving to Thirsk grammar school at the age of 11.

Nothing particularly dramatic occurred there - until one day he fell victim to typhoid fever, and lost quite a lot of ground in his studies.

"I remember that on the way home I was conscious of a burning sensation in my throat, and a kind of buzzing in my ears, as well as a frightful headache. When I got home I was immediately sent to bed. The doctor was called in and confirmed that I had typhoid.

"I was confined to bed for 13 weeks, during which time I was constantly delirious, and remember little about what was going on round me. I vaguely recall people fussing round me, and by the time I recovered I was like a skeleton. Aunt Neilie (on my mother's side) came to see me shortly afterwards, and didn't exactly help by shrieking, 'Oh my God - just look at Willy!'

The fever left me with an inherent weakness, which lasted for years, and also led to one of the most traumatic periods of my life."

Before this event occurred, however, ten-year-old Bill had experienced his first encounter with death. It happened while the family were on holiday in Scarborough, and because he was so young he had to share a bedroom with his grandmother.

Bill still remembers the incident vividly. "Late in the evening I was woken up by a bump, and there was Grandma, who was 65, lying on the floor beside the bed. She was very still, and being a child, I flew into a panic. I called out for my mother, who came running in, but Grandma died soon afterwards.

"An inquest had to be held, conducted by the Scarborough coroner, about which I remember very little, except that I was worried, because I thought I might have accidentally pushed her out of bed. However, that was ruled out.

"The coroner adjourned the hearing, because apparently Grandma had suffered some bruising, and he was anxious to get to the bottom of this.

"At the resumed inquest, at which I was called to give evidence, he cross-examined Mother so intensely that it eventually led to her having a nervous breakdown. No doubt the coroner was only doing his job, but it led to a lot of ill-feeling, and our MP was actually called in to inquire into the circumstances. To me, however, he was quite polite. He shook me tightly by the hand and said," Nice to see you, Willy".

"I assume that a 'natural causes' verdict was reached, but Mother was so traumatised by what she had gone through, that she fell ill and returned to Cumbria, where she stayed with relatives for several months. During this time we three children went to stay with relatives.

"I remember looking at a newspaper report of the proceedings sometime later, but Mother snatched it away. 'That's not the sort of thing you should be reading.' she snapped, which really was not like her.

He never found the report again, and a trawl through the archives of the Darlington & Stockton Times has revealed nothing.

Bill stayed at Thirsk grammar school for a total of three years, but was considerably weakened by the typhoid attack, and his parents decided that he would be better off breathing sea air. Accordingly, they packed him off to boarding school in Scarborough, to the bewilderment of their eldest son.

The shy, sensitive youth was totally unequipped for the Spartan regime he found there - 46 miles from home in an institution which was distinctly short on benevolence.

"I suddenly realised what a sheltered life I'd led, whereas, to me, that school was straight out of the pages of Dickens - harsh and unrelenting, with only the friendship of a few masters and pupils to alleviate it.

"Things became so bad that I would go to bed, praying that I wouldn't wake up to face the following day. These were undoubtedly the darkest days of my life.

"I can never forget the first savage beating I received. I had done nothing whatsoever to deserve it. A boy sitting at the desk behind me said something which I didn't catch, so I turned round to hear better.

"Immediately I was pounced upon; accused of cheating, although no exams were in progress, and hauled in front of the headmaster.

"In vain I protested that I had done nothing. He flatly refused to listen. My trousers were pulled down, and I received no fewer than 15 strokes of the cane. 'Six of the best' would have been kind by comparison.

"It was the worst beating of my life, and the sheer injustice of it was compounded by another master, who sniggered, 'You won't be able to sit down now, will you, Foggitt?'"

Bill reflected on what would have happened if he had been subject to such an onslaught today. "That headmaster would probably have been in court on a charge of causing actual bodily harm, but in those days it was useless to complain: the teachers were always in the right.

"Incidentally," he went on, "the headmaster had the gall to nickname me 'Solemnsides'. Did he expect me to be a 'laughingsides' after treatment like that?"

His face clouded over as he recalled falling from the wall bars of the gymnasium, and not being able to get up. "All the PE master could bellow was, 'Get up, get up. What do you think you are - a little monkey?'

"Another time a sadistic master took hold of a small boy by his ears, and twisted them until he screamed with pain. Several boys tried to escape, and I wish I'd had the courage to join them. Two were found shivering in a seafront shelter the following morning, and another was recaptured on the back of a lorry on the outskirts of the resort.

"They certainly paid for their initiative when they got back to school."

Bill's face creased in a smile, however, when he recalled the head's discomfiture over a gas leak. He said the incident left him with an overwhelming sense of satisfaction, and had, in a sense, evened up the score.

"Some of the pupils were larking around, kicking a ball around in the dormitory. One of them sent it flying into one of the gas lamps, setting up an ominous hissing. It wasn't quite dark and not one of the lamps was lit.

"The next we knew, an aged factotum came rushing in, carrying a lighted taper. The man must have been stupid. What was wrong with his sense of smell? Or perhaps he was hoping to ignite whichever lamp was leaking. Whatever he was thinking, seconds later the head followed him in, screaming, "Stop, stop - you'll blow us all up!" He was in a monumental panic, and we were in a state of euphoria. Somehow I felt that the head's cowardice evened up the score between us.

"Afterwards the boy who kicked the ball became something of a hero, and we nicknamed him 'Gassy' Brundrett."

It was while he was at Scarborough that Bill learned about the secrets of seaweed. He would often walk along the beach, and at first didn't pay any attention to the heaps of sea wrack which lay in his path. After a while, however, he became aware of its crispness in dry weather, and the fact that it degenerated into a slimy mass when the weather was unsettled and moist.

It was only later that he discovered the scientific reason for this, and it was this knowledge which helped to make him famous 40 years later, when he started making regular appearances on Yorkshire Television.

Bill was an average sportsman during his schooldays. He particularly liked playing cricket, once scoring 35 runs, the best innings in his short career as a batsman. He detested football, however, but added, "However, it was lucky for me that we didn't play Rugby; I would have been torn apart."

Bill has been back to his old school in recent years. "It is now co-educational and the atmosphere has changed completely. The staff were extremely kind and glad to show me round, but I couldn't repress a shudder when I saw a picture of my former headmaster on the wall."

He left the school in 1931 in a much better frame of mind than when he entered it.

His father died in 1962 on a bitterly cold day, in Thirsk market place. "My mother had begged him not to go out, reminding him about his heart condition, but father was always stubborn, and said he would be all right.

"He collapsed from a heart attack, and as he lay dying, his last words were, 'Please look after my dog.' That was typical of him. He really loved his dogs. Looking back, with the belated understanding which comes with maturity, I can see that, for all his strictures, he was essentially a kind person, and his death was a great loss to the town."

Mr Foggitt was 81 when he died. His widow survived him by 15 years, and Bill paid her this tribute, "She was a warm, loving person. Not demonstrative, but with a quiet determination to ensure that we were brought up in an atmosphere of security and love. When she died in 1977, my sense of loss was overwhelming, and Betty Cook was a tower of strength.

"Quite a few people thought her aloof, and I am sure that reserved people often bring that sort of criticism on their heads. But, in fact, Mother was a good mixer, and loved going to whist drives. She also enjoyed her garden, and like all true countrywomen was an excellent cook.

"She bought a car before the war, and would drive members of the family and friends all over the place. She once let me take the wheel, before the days of licences, but seeing a lorry approaching, I panicked and hit a grassy bank - fortunately without doing any damage.

"That was enough for me. I never got behind a wheel again, although I bought a motor cycle for £5, and drove it for a few years before selling it for £1."

Bill's Grandfather, Benjamin Foggitt: Fellow of the Linnaean Society.

W. FOGGITT & SONS

Chemists

Cameras and Photographic Goods
Developing and Printing a Speciality

Agricultural, Horticultural
and Dairy Requisites

Sponges, Tooth Brushes and
other Toilet Requisites

ooo0(●0ooo

HORSE MEDICINES
VETERINARY CLINICALS etc

ooo0(●0ooo

MARKET PLACE, THIRSK

Advert for W. Foggitt and Son, Chemists, from a pre-2nd World War
Guide to Thirsk.

Bill's parents, Elizabeth and Benjamin Foggitt.

In Loving Memory of
WILLIAM FOGGITT. F.L.S.
who Died MAY 10ᵀᴴ 1917
AGED 82 YEARS.
Also of
ELIZABETH T. FOGGITT
wife of the above,
who Died MARCH 1ˢᵀ 1905
AGED 63 YEARS.
AND OF
LOUISA ANNE HALL,
DAUGHTER OF THE ABOVE,
who Died OCTOBER 26ᵀᴴ 1918
AGED 40 YEARS.

Louisa Anne Hall, who fled from her husband's hotel with a customer, and who was said to have gone down with the "Titanic", is buried in her father's grave in Thirsk cemetery. Her death is wrongly inscribed as 1918.

CERTIFIED COPY OF AN ENTRY OF DEATH

GIVEN AT THE GENERAL REGISTER OFFICE

Application Number W 008205

REGISTRATION DISTRICT Islington

1916. DEATH in the Sub-district of Islington South East in the County of London

No.	When and where died	Name and surname	Sex	Age	Occupation	Cause of death	Signature, description and residence of informant	When registered	Signature of registrar
Columns:-	1	2	3	4	5	6	7	8	9
207	Twenty-sixth October 1916 The London Hospital Liverpool Road	Louisa Anne Stall	Female	40 years	Stanley Hotel, 21 London Street, Paddington, wife of William Webbancroft Hotel Proprietor	Constrictive bowel, Syphilitic Prescriptions, 5 days, Cardiac failure, 2 days, Certified by Francis Gartland Nicholson M.D.	Ada Tennant sister in attendance Falie de House, Roode, Yorkshire	Twenty-ninth October 1916	James Dunnit Registrar.

CERTIFIED to be a true copy of an entry in the certified copy of a Register of Deaths in the District above mentioned.

Given at the GENERAL REGISTER OFFICE, under the Seal of the said Office, the 2nd day of December 1963

The proof. Aunt Louisa's death certificate proving that she died in 1916.

47

Seeking insiration. . . Bill completed a course in pelmanism to help him with his pharmaceutical examination.

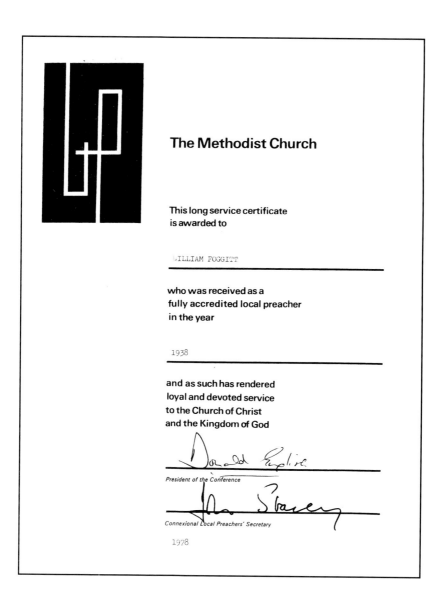

The Methodist Church

This long service certificate
is awarded to

WILLIAM FOGGITT

who was received as a
fully accredited local preacher
in the year

1938

and as such has rendered
loyal and devoted service
to the Church of Christ
and the Kingdom of God

President of the Conference

Connexional Local Preachers' Secretary

1978

Bill's long service certificate as a local preacher with the Methodist Church.

49

N⁰ 567

St. David's College, Lampeter.

WE, The Principal, Tutors and Professors of ST. DAVID'S COLLEGE, HEREBY CERTIFY that _William Foggitt_ of this College _B.A._ has been a resident Member of this College for _Twelve_ Terms, _Four_ Years, between _October 1939_ and _March 1946_ during which time he has conducted himself to our satisfaction, and has passed all the Examinations required for the _Pass_ course.

IN WITNESS WHEREOF we have hereunto subscribed our names this _13_ day of _March_, 1946

A Certificate in Pastoral Subjects is issued by the College, and it is requested that it should be required of all Students who are seeking Ordination.

H.K. Archdall M.A. Th. Soc. Principal.
A.A. Harris M.A. Professor
W.H. Harris, M.A., B.Litt, Senior Tutor.
D. Dawson. B.A. Th. Litt. Professor
W.H. Morgan BA, BD. Lecturer.
E.C. Rowlands, M.A. M.B.E. Chaplain & Tutor
F.J.T. David, M.A. Chaplain & Tutor.
F.R. Newte. B.A. Lecturer.

A measure of success with the church of England, sadly not to last.

50

CHAPTER 4

A YOUNG MAN'S FANCY LIGHTLY TURNS TO THOUGHTS OF LOVE

It was while he was nearing the end of his time at boarding school that Bill experienced his first romance.

It was a world away from the informal, relaxed meeting of minds - and it must be said, bodies - of today, where in towns and cities and least, innocence is derided, and clever young people try to jump fences ever more confidently in the early development stakes. There are no handicaps.

In Bill's younger days, pure femininity was a girl's best, and only, way of achieving equality. They didn't think of driving cars or lorries, boxing, wrestling, giving orders on the boardroom floor, or becoming front-line combatants.

For the most part they were demure creatures, deserving of protection and respect, and most boys tended to show them this.

The authority of their parents was paramount.

Today's generation would say they were repressed. And, to be fair, they probably were. Life was lived within a tight social framework, and woe betide a girl who became pregnant. She was stigmatised forever.

Had it been different, no doubt the girls would have exercised their freedom in a similar way to their granddaughters.

However, such thoughts were unheard of when Bill first approached a bank manager's daughter when he was 17, and timorously asked if she would like to go out. Audrey Cooper was a vivacious, wholesome girl, whose father ran the bank next door to the Foggitt establishment.

Like Bill, she had a refreshing sense of humour, which belied her serious side.

She was studying for university when she and Bill first started "walking out", which was an apt phrase, because it was in walking that the young couple found a natural meeting point.

Both had an abiding interest in flowers and the little creatures they encountered on their ramblings, which were often concentrated around Helmsley, 14 miles across the Hambleton Hills, to which market town they travelled by bus.

They laughed and giggled their way round the magnificent ruins of Rievaulx Abbey, and along the banks of the River Rye, occasionally stealing a shy kiss when there was nobody in the vicinity.

With misty eyes Bill revived memories of those golden days in the sun, "To me, Audrey was like one of nature's most beautiful flowers. We had wonderful conversations, ranging from plants and flowers to religion. She was a very religious girl. Once we were strolling alongside the river, and I plucked up the courage to ask her if she loved me.

"What a thrill I experienced when she shyly told me she did, and mischievously I asked whether she loved me enough to jump into the water for me.

"I can hear her reply now as clearly as I did then. Rather bashfully, she replied, 'Yes, if you really wanted me to do.'

On another occasion she confided in me that she had prayed for my success in the school certificate examination.

She gave me a photograph of herself, which I carried round with me for nearly 60 years until it finally disintegrated. She also gave me a four-leafed clover - a rarity which is supposed to bring luck - murmuring to me, 'This is for you, forever.'

"Was I truly in love, or was I in love with love? How can I possibly imagine what might have happened if we had married, and had to face up to harsh realities? I prefer not to speculate, and that way the memories remain forever fresh and beautiful in my mind.

"Nearly 70 years on, Audrey is still the love of my life.

"But they day inevitably came when we had to part. Audrey's father was moved to Driffield, in the East Riding of Yorkshire. Parting was agony, and although we both promised to keep in touch, we gradually drifted apart.

"Audrey duly went to London University, where she met and married a fellow-student.

"They had two children. Then, in 1941 a bombshell hit me. At the age of only 28, Audrey died. I don't know exactly how it happened, but I heard it was the outcome of an operation that went wrong. Although it was some years since we had met, I was absolutely devastated. A precious flower had broken before the wind.

"Later, I cycled something like 50 miles to Driffield to see her grave. Standing there in the cemetery I was seized by a great melancholy, and tears flowed for the dream that never materialised."

After Audrey's death, a strange thing happened. Bill often used to dream about her, and one night she appeared in his sleep, and told him her husband had died.

After a lapse of time, Bill had all but forgotten his dream, when he chanced to pick up a copy of the Yorkshire Post.

It carried a report of Audrey's husband - killed in a riding accident.

Bill mused, "Whether the dream was the result of an over-fertile imagination, or Audrey was actually speaking to me from another place, I haven't the slightest idea, but whatever it was, it proved to be a grim prophesy."

Without Audrey's refreshing personality to inspire him, and being stuck in the family chemist's shop as a humble, unqualified assistant, without any prospects, he became steadily more restless and fretful.

The Methodist religion proved to be the palliative he was seeking. Since boyhood he had looked upon the chapel as an important part of his life. Being made to attend services had not soured him; he loved the robust hymn singing, together with the simplicity of the church's message, and the fellowship of meetings.

He struck up a friendship with the Reverend Leslie Hayes, who had arrived in Thirsk as a probationer minister, and together they found common ground in walking and a love of the countryside.

They would embark on hiking tours covering several days, and engage in animated discussions, particularly about religion and nature. As we shall see, these treks sometimes led them into dramatic situations.

It was during this period that Bill began to think about becoming a Methodist local preacher. He was excellent at English and had a good turn of phrase to back up his faith, as well as being conversant with the Bible.

He also had a great admiration for that band of dedicated laymen, who preached from the heart, and walked miles to take Sunday services, although they were not ordained. They were drawn from all walks of life, and often their shortfalls were far outweighed by the sheer fervour of their message.

In addition to augmenting the church's often over-stretched resources, many of them became extremely popular because of their powerful, sometimes inspired, oratory, which often rivalled that of the ministers themselves.

"To me, however," Bill recalled, "their informal and relaxed way of putting religious points across added interest to services, and showed the Methodist church at its best. I certainly believe that the church nowadays needs an injection of this sort of spirit. It grieves me to see congregations dwindling, and churches being closed and turned into warehouses."

It was when he went to Biggleswade that he realised he hadn't escaped his father's beady eye.

"I was extremely surprised when the local Methodist minister came up and introduced himself, saying how nice it was to meet me. At first I wondered what he was talking about, and how he came to know about me. He explained that my father had contacted him, and asked him to keep an eye on me. Perhaps he thought I would abuse my new-found freedom - on the pay of a chemist's assistant!

"As it happened the minister and I became firm friends, and it was he who pointed out the magnificent display of the northern lights in 1938, while I came across equally illuminating acquaintance at local fellowship meetings."

When he returned to Thirsk, Bill was even more determined to become a local preacher, and told the Methodist minister about his ambition.

To his astonishment, the worthy gentleman, who did not enjoy the best of health, replied, "Grand - you can start by taking the service at Knayton (a village on the A19, north of Thirsk) on Sunday. I don't feel up to it myself."

For a moment Bill stood, open-mouthed, at the easy informality with which he was being invited to realised his ambition. "I must have looked quite comical," he said, "but I seized my chance eagerly, even though I hadn't had any formal training, and duly delivered my first address to a rather startled congregation.

"However, I knew my Bible, and could speak pretty fluently, so I was able to put together a passable address, although I can't for the life of me remember what it was about.

"But the congregation seemed pleased enough, and after that I took several services in the Thirsk area. I was often complimented, and it was then that the idea of becoming a properly ordained minster came into my head.

"I went through the normal channels, and in due course was put forward as a candidate. I was quite confident about my chances, but to my extreme surprise and disappointment, my preaching didn't come up to what the district synod at Malton was looking for, although they were quite satisfied with my written work.

"It was a bitter blow. My future as a chemist's assistant seemed bleak. I had failed my school certificate, and pharmaceutical examination, and had no qualifications. The family shop had been sold to Boots, so what on earth was I to do?"

Not for the first time, it was his mother who came up with a solution."Why not try to become a minister in the Church of England?" she asked, adding that she would have a word with the vicar of Sowerby, the Reverend G D John, to see if he could put me in touch with the appropriate people.

"Fortunately," said Bill, "he knew about my preaching and knowledge of the Bible and the scriptures, and as a result of his intervention I found myself accepted for the Theological College at Lampeter, in Wales.

"By this time war was almost upon us, and the college itself had closed, although lectures were held in private houses which it owned. It was a nice little college, and everyone was extremely courteous, but we seemed to spend as much time being drilled by a couple of lecturers for the Home Guard, as we did on lectures.

"It was really quite chaotic, because both lecturers and students were being called up, but I managed to get a degree in divinity in two years, rather than the usual three, because of this.

"I was at the college for three years, from 1939 to 1942, by which time all able-bodied men were required for the armed forces.

"In due course I found myself reporting for duty at the RAOC headquarters in the midlands. Actually, I was quite relieved to be getting into uniform, but I still feel rather bitter about those trainees who escaped the call-up and were duly ordained, whereas I had to soldier on until 1946, and eventually failed to become a priest."

Bill's diaries record in detail the hopes and agonies which accompanied his efforts to complete his training on his return to the college, leading up to his failure to pass the General Certificate of Ordination.

The passage of time has a mellowing effect, however, and Bill gradually realised he simply wasn't cut out for the cloth. "It seemed like a great goal at the time, but I honestly believe I would not have made a success as a Church of England vicar, so it's perhaps as well that I was eventually rejected. I think, on balance, however, that I would have made the grade as a Methodist minister."

But Bill's problems did not lie solely with his own personality. They also had their roots in his affection for a vicar's daughter whom he met at a local dance, several years before the war.

When war came, they agreed to keep in touch with each other, and corresponded throughout much of the conflict. Within months of Bill being demobbed in 1946, they found themselves walking up the aisle together, and Bill then returned to continue his studies at Lampeter.

As a result, the marriage underwent considerable financial strain, and Bill found himself wondering whether he was doing the right thing. Doubts and mental conflicts began to assail him, undermining his resolve, and were ultimately equally to blame for his failure.

The story of the marriage that was entered in haste, and repented at leisure, will be referred to in a later chapter.

Before falling in with Bill's army career, an incident in 1933, which came about as a result of his walking tours with Leslie Hayes, deserves to be highlighted, because it carries a warning for the inexperienced hiker nearly 70 years later.

It also taught the future weather expert a lesson which his great-grandfather had divined one hundred years previously: never take the English weather for granted, especially towards the end of a long, dry spell.

It was a deluge, ironically enough, in that same area of Cross Fell where the great storm of 1771 that devastated Yarm, was spawned, that took Bill and Leslie completely unawares, and could have had disastrous consequences.

As it was, it brought Bill to his knees with exhaustion. Had he been alone in that wilderness of featureless grass and moorland, he might even have died, and only his companion's strong right arm steered him to safety.

Anyone who has walked the High Cup Nick area above Teesdale, will vouch for its dangers when snow, mist or heavy rain, blot out visibility.

But during the heatwave of 1933, when the formidable slopes were bathed in sunshine, and the River Tees was reduced to little more than a trickle, Bill and Leslie were blissfully ignorant of what they were letting themselves in for, as they headed for Cross Fell.

At one point they were warned by a cafe owner that the dry spell was beginning to break up, but in the arrogance of youth they strode on, regardless, up the valley of the Tees.

Leslie, a precise young man who never wasted words, was supremely fit, and exuded the confidence of a natural leader, while Bill still suffered from the inherent weakness of his typhoid illness.

For him, walking was considered therapeutic; a way of rebuilding his strength.

As the two men began to leave farmhouses and barns behind them, they hardly noticed the black clouds gathering above them, until suddenly, with a sinister hiss, the first raindrops fell. Within minutes they were engulfed in a torrential downpour.

The heatwave had ended - and their ordeal was about to begin.

Visibility closed in; temperatures plummeted, and as they plodded upwards, they were forced to follow the course of the river. This in itself was taking a risk, as anglers in particular can testify.

Heavy rain can transform Pennine streams into raging torrents in a magically short space of time. Walls of water build up and race down valleys, like the Severn bore in reverse, and many a fisherman in the lower reaches has been taken by surprise and drowned.

Luckily Bill and Leslie did not have to face this hazard, but soaked to the skin, they were becoming increasingly tired and worried. Said Bill, "I can't recollect much about that terrible trek. We just plodded on and on through the wilderness, and I think I must have been close to passing out several times. Everything was blurred in a curtain of rain, and it was only Leslie who kept me going. I wouldn't have had the strength to continue if I hadn't had him to lean on.

"The one thing I do remember, however, is the haunting cry of curlews, like the souls of the dead, mocking me. Bloody curlews ...!

"And then, just when it seemed that I couldn't go on, Leslie let out a shout, and there in the distance we could just make out a light through the pouring rain. We stumbled towards it, and I think it must have been about midnight when we staggered up to the door of a farmhouse.

"We knocked, and it was opened by two ladies, who couldn't believe their eyes when they looked at our dripping forms. Apparently one was the mother, who was visiting her daughter and son-in-law, and their children.

"One of them told us it was lucky we had found them up at that time, but not having seen each other for a long time they were busy chatting, and hadn't noticed the clock.

"Anyway, they dried us out and actually moved the children to make up a bed for us. They made us a hot drink, and we explained how we came to be there. We then enjoyed a good night's sleep, and in the morning, after an excellent breakfast, set out for Cross Fell in perfect weather.

"The women wouldn't hear of taking any money from us, so we slipped some into the pockets of the children's coats, which were hanging up behind a door. We had told our hostesses where we came from, and you can imagine how surprised and gratified I was to receive a hamper of food from them, as a gesture of thanks for leaving the money."

Bill added, "I have seldom received such hospitality. We could have been a couple of desperados for all they knew, yet they didn't hesitate to invite us in. I believe the daughter's husband was away at the time."

Bill has recently been back to High Force in Teesdale, where they set out from on that fateful day, and while there, sent a postcard to Leslie, who was in a wheelchair and living in Cornwall.

However, laconic as ever, he replied, "It doesn't change much, does it?"

On another occasion, the intrepid pair were confronted by a drama of a different sort while walking Hadrian's Wall.

They were relying on getting accommodation in farmhouses. "We were hot and tired," said Bill, "and were getting a bit worried about a finding somewhere to stay, when he spotted this isolated farm.

"As was his habit, Leslie went boldly up to the front door, and knocked loudly.

"Suddenly an upstairs window was pulled up, and to our astonishment, a woman confronted us with a shotgun. 'Who are you, and what do you want here?' she demanded." She was cross-eyed and I remembering wondering which of us she would hit if she let fly.

"Cool as ever, Leslie turned to me and commented, 'What an extraordinary reception' before explaining to the woman that we were merely seeking a night's accommodation. He explained that we were walking the wall, and would be happy to pay her what she wanted.

"Well, the gun was lowered and the lady let us in. She was most apologetic, explaining that escaped prisoners from a nearby jail sometimes passed that way, and she couldn't be too careful.

"As we ate an excellent meal, she added that she lived on her own.

"All I can say is that she must have had the courage of a lioness to have lived there under those circumstances. It must have been bad enough, being on her own, but having escaped prisoners to put up with must have tested her nerves to breaking point."

The walking tours eventually came to an end when Leslie was ordained and left Thirsk for South Shields.

However, they continued to maintain contact until Leslie's death in 1999.

CHAPTER 5

ARMY LIFE: PRIVATE FOGGITT MUDDLES THROUGH

B ill was conscripted in 1942 on the day the Duke of Kent was killed in an aircraft crash in Scotland.

He was abruptly transplanted from the courtesy and comfortable surroundings of Lampeter into the rigorous reality of a country at war.

The fact that he was training to be a priest cut no ice with the non-commissioned officers entrusted with the task of transforming pimply-faced, knock-kneed youths into rugged fighting men.

From the moment he walked through the gates of the Royal Army Ordnance Corps depot, his individualism was swallowed up in a featureless agglomeration of bewildered humanity, and he simply became Private Foggitt, RAOC, property of the armed forces of His Majesty the King.

The coarseness of his khaki uniform, staccato commands, and doing almost everything at the double, came as a rude shock to his system, as did the Spartan conditions of the barrack room.

And, being one of those unfortunate people whom adversity seems to single out, it was inevitable that Bill was soon in trouble.

Bemused by the simplest forms of technology, he found himself in a tussle with a piece of cord, known as a pull-through, and a fragment of flannel known as four-by-two, which fitted through a loop at the end of the cord.

A few drops of oil were added to the four-by-two, and the contraption was then pulled through the barrel of the .303 Lee Enfield rifle, removing every trace of grit which might have accumulated.

Quite a simple operation, you'd think, but Bill had to be the one man in the British army who couldn't get it right. Somehow the pull-through became stuck in the barrel, and after dashing out on to the parade ground, he was forced to present the rifle for inspection with the cord sticking out of the barrel.

As he presented the weapon, it whipped past the sergeant's face like an angry snake.

"God," the big man bellowed. "That nearly had my eye out. What's that thing doing, still in your rifle?"

Flustered and panicking, Bill was immediately put on a charge - he can't remember what it was - and within a week of setting out to fight for his country, was sentenced to three days CB (confined to barracks).

He recalled the officer who handed out the punishment. "He told me the sentence was light because I obviously came from a good home, and looked after my things. But then I jumped when he roared, "Well, you'll have to learn to do the same thing here. March him out.""

Bill added, "CB was more than just being confined to barracks. You had to parade outside the guardroom in full kit, and I even had to get help to assemble this. Then you had to carry out any jobs allocated to you. One of my tasks was to scrub the guardroom floor, and I remember an NCO sitting in a chair with his arm round a woman, making sarcastic comments. Don't ask me what a female was doing there: maybe she was in the army herself.

"That NCO obviously thought it very funny when he 'accidentally' kicked over the bucket of water I was using."

However, although Bill didn't fit in with the image of a fighting soldier, he had one saving grace - he turned out to be an excellent shot. His marksmanship soon attracted the attention of the officer in charge of the firing range, who would remark, "Nice shooting, Foggitt. You're doing well. Keep it up."

"Naturally I was very pleased, but was quickly brought down to earth. When I got back to the barrack room one day, one of those sturdy characters you meet in the army, the sort who could never recite Shakespeare, but could worm his way into the Royal enclosure at Ascot, gave me some alarming advice.

"Whether it was based on fact or not, I never found out, but the gist of it was that I was being singled out for a sniper's job, and that, he added, was just about the most dangerous job in the army.

"After that, the range officer became more and more perplexed as my shooting inexplicably veered off target. I haven't a clue as to what would have happened if I hadn't been given that advice. It may have been a joke to prevent me becoming big-headed, but, of course, I was too naive to contemplate this at the time.

"In any case, it wasn't worth the risk. It may be all very well to be able to shoot a fly through the eye, but imagine Private Bill Foggitt, who couldn't harm a field mouse, stuck up a tree or bombed-out building, training a Lee Enfield, capable of killing a man a mile away, on some unsuspecting German soldier, and shooting him down in cold blood.

"Even in wartime that sort of thing didn't appeal to me, and more to the point, the life of the sniper is usually very short."

Bill was posted to Tripoli after the decisive battle of El Alamein, and found his way into a comfortable office job.

He struck up a friendship with a vicar's son, and the pair regularly attended religious meetings organised by the padre. With his knowledge of the scriptures, Bill was quickly accepted as a valuable member of the group, and this was to prove invaluable a short time later.

It happened when Bill unaccountably split his shirt. Normally, army personnel become skilled at repairs to kit, darning socks and ironing their battledress with the aid of damped brown paper.

Whether Bill would have measured up in this department is not clear, but in any case, a sergeant who had obviously been waiting for just such an opportunity, gave him no chance. "'Abuse of kit, Private Foggitt,' he bellowed in my ear", and promptly put me on a charge.

"Now this was a pretty trivial incident, and the charge thoroughly unwarranted. In fact, it hardly deserved to be called an offence, but this sergeant had it in for me. Perhaps he was jealous of my sinecure in the office, and my rapport with the padre.

"Anyway, I was duly marched in to the regimental office, where, by a stroke of luck, the presiding officer was none other than the padre.

I suppose in civilian circles he would have had to declare an 'interest' in the case and retired, but the army has its own way of doing things - or at any rate, it did in wartime."

The charge was duly read out, and the padre, who was obviously irritated by the pettiness of it, turned to me and said, 'Now Willy, what's the problem?'

"After I had explained the situation, he turned to an obviously angry sergeant, and told him to set the charge aside. 'There's no problem,' he told me. 'Just go to the stores and get yourself another shirt.'

"I thought that sergeant would have a fit of apoplexy when the padre added as an aside, 'By the way Willy, will you be at our next meeting?'

"When we got outside, he muttered through clenched teeth, 'You'd get away with bloody murder, Foggitt.'

"I made sure I was disappearing over the horizon whenever he hove into view after that."

The army has many sinecures for those clever enough to spot them. Opportunism is a sure passport for a 'cushy number.' Censoring mail might be said to fit into this category, and the officer with the task of rooting out potential subversives, was obviously bored to tears in his little office.

One day he sent for Bill, whose letters home were, by comparison with others, models of erudition. "He told me he had read these, and was quite apologetic. He had noted my references to the Bible, and obviously regarded me as being totally incapable of upskittling the British war machine.

"He wanted me to be his right-hand man in epistle-evaluating, and this gave me a wonderfully comfortable job. Nowadays, all I can remember about him was that he kept going on about not realising the Children of Israel had got as far as Tripoli.

"Well, to the best of my knowledge, I knew that the tribes had never ventured in a western direction, but I suppose a desert is a desert, whether it be the Libyan or the Sinai, so I didn't bother to correct him.

"He was terribly bored, I felt, and just wanted someone like me to talk to. Perhaps in his mind's eye, he would have been better shooting fleeing Germans from an armoured car."

'By this time, the war drums were receding, and Bill was posted to Cairo. During 1944, the padre arranged a trip to the Holy Land, inviting Bill and the vicar's son along.

Recollection of the flight, however, still gives Bill a queasy feeling. "The turbulence was vicious, and threw the plane about like a cork. I thought we were sure to crash, and everyone except the vicar's son, was thoroughly ill. However, whereas the others quickly recovered, once on the ground, I, of course, was much worse, and had to be carried from the aircraft, but it was a small price to pay for having been delivered.

"On Easter Sunday we attended a service conducted by the Anglican bishop of Jerusalem, which I found singularly uninspiring, and were then taken to see the place on the road to Emmaus, where Jesus appeared to his disciples after the resurrection. Frankly, I was again unimpressed.

"Perhaps I had expected too much of the Holy Land. This dry, dusty road certainly needed the risen Christ to give it any significance. As it was, the only thing which appealed to me was a sign advertising Jaffa oranges for sale.

"My spirits were considerably uplifted by those huge, juicy Jaffas, and I can only hope my lack of respect has been made up for during my subsequent years as a preacher."

While stationed in Cairo, Bill was for a time helping to guard army equipment which was stored in caves. "An odd incident occurred while I was in there," he recalled.

"It only lasted a few seconds, but because it was so weird, it has lived on in my memory.

"There I was, kicking my heels, when out of the darkness a strange figure appeared.

"I suppose he was a soldier, although I can't remember whether he was wearing a uniform. He just stopped; looked at me, and without explanation recited the words, 'I'm a little prairie flower, growing wilder by the hour; nobody wants to cultivate me, because I'm as wild as wild can be.'

"With that he turned on his heel and disappeared into the gloom, leaving me dumbfounded. You certainly meet some queer folk in the army, but few, I suspect, so odd as this apparition.

"Maybe he was a budding poet, or had had a touch of the sun. At any rate, I made a point of remembering the couplet, but have never come across it since."

Just when the British were looking forward to returning to Blighty, they found themselves caught up in another vicious little war, involving Jews, Arabs and the army.

Ironically, this conflict posed a greater threat to Bill than the desert war, in which he had never heard a shell fired in anger.

Bill duly saw his name on a list of postings to Palestine while in Cairo. He and his rifle should have travelled together, but somehow he had managed to mislay the weapon.

"I hadn't a clue where I had put it down, and there was this sergeant shouting, 'Come on, come on, get along there, there's no time to lose. Get fell in and get on the truck.' or words to that effect. 'By the way, Foggitt, what's happened to your rifle?' I told him I seemed to have mislaid it, but he cut me short, shouting, 'All right - never mind the bloody thing - just get moving.'"

In so doing, he laid up a store of trouble for one of the army's most naive soldiers.

"That's the story of my life," sighed Bill. "I was always a bit of a scatterbrain. I just scrambled on to the truck, little knowing that some of the most anxious days of my life lay ahead."

With that, he was once again on the way to the Holy Land, in less pleasurable circumstances than before." Our war was drawing to a close, but in this little corner of the world, the Jews were fighting for a homeland, and murdering British soldiers in the process.

"The first thing we did on reporting to our new base in Tel Aviv, was to hand in our weapons at the armoury. When my turn came, and I told them I had lost my rifle in Egypt, there was a horrified silence, almost as if I's shouted 'Heil Hitler!'

"Whether the staff thought I was being a little bit casual about it, I don't know. But I was brought up with a jerk when they warned me, 'You'll be hearing more of this, Private Foggitt!'

"Sure enough, it was not long before I was charged with losing the weapon, and really started to worry when a little chap, a staunch Roman Catholic, crossed himself, and a corporal muttered something about it being a capital offence in wartime.

"My imagination began to take over. I remembered an uncle, who had been on the Somme during the First World War, telling me about two 17 year-olds who had been executed for throwing away their kit, and despite the heat, I went all goosefleshy.

"A firing squad? Inoffensive Willy Foggitt being blindfolded and led out at dawn to pay the ultimate price? For an offence which that sergeant in Cairo had dismissed so lightly?

"Of course, deep down I didn't' really believe it could happen, but the mind plays funny tricks, and I couldn't be absolutely sure. I thought it best to believe the worst, in the hope of being proved wrong.

"Uncle had said the boys in the trenches had been shell-shocked - yet I had never heard the sound of an enemy shell during the whole time I was on active service so that could hardly apply to me.

"I was so worried, I couldn't eat properly, and then, a fortnight later, the summons came. After a brief hearing, I was marched outside to where two burly military policemen were waiting beside a jeep. I was ordered into the vehicle, and then we roared of to Haifa, 60 miles to the north.

"I tried to keep my spirits up by making light conversation. 'Lovely country, isn't it?' I ventured. Instantly two weapons were trained on my chest. Those redcaps didn't say a word. Their faces seemed to be carved out of granite, and I fell silent.

"After that, it became an extremely uncomfortable journey.

"On arrival, I was taken down some steps to a cell, and pushed through a door with a huge iron handle. I prayed all that night, and my fear must have showed on my fact the following morning, because the sergeant who told me I was to be questioned added, 'Don't worry lad, everything will be all right.'

"Those were some of the most comforting words I ever heard.

"Then I was marched into an office, where a burly officer sat, head in hands.

"My knees were like jelly as I awaited the dreaded words ... 'Private Foggitt, you have committed one of the most serious offences in the military handbook ... ' or something of the sort.

But, as it happened, no such indictment was forthcoming. Instead, to my utmost astonishment, he merely told me that losing a rifle was a serious offence, and I would have to be punished.

"However, he followed up by saying I could either accept his punishment, which meant I would not be court-martialled, or if I chose, I could go before the higher court. Needless to say, I didn't hesitate.

"Then to my surprise he said I would have to pay for the rifle, and asked for my pay-book. I told him I didn't have enough money, and he said that was all right - the army would put me in credit, and the cost of the Lee Enfield would come out of that.

"I can't remember how much the rifle cost, and in any case it didn't matter.

"I was marched out into the sunshine, a feeling of untold relief overwhelming me.

"On the way back I tried to tell the redcaps about my deliverance, but their reactions were depressingly similar. Their weapons were once again pointed at me, and the ebullient Private Foggitt shrank under their cold stares.

"When I got back to Tel Aviv, my Catholic friend actually shed tears. He had not expected to see me again."

Soon after this, Bill had a narrow escape from eternity.

He was going off guard duty, and making his way from the guardroom, when there was a terrific explosion, and debris rained down on him. "Luckily," said Bill, "I had turned a corner of the building, and was to some extent protected from the blast, which could not have been more than a minute after I had left the guardroom.

"The guard commander, I believe, was killed. All I recollect was seeing a load of rubble and smoke, and getting out as quickly as possible. It was a terrorist bomb, but who had planted it, Jew or Arab, I never knew. It certainly shook my morale, and made me realise this was no phoney war.

"I shivered when I realised how close to death I had been, and as on many other occasions, felt someone was looking after me.

"Then there was a time when I suppose I could have been charged with dereliction of duty. I was on guard duty, when I saw a man dressed like Lawrence of Arabia coming towards me. There was nothing furtive about his approach, and I was so taken aback that I just gaped and completely forgot to challenge him.

"I thought it must be someone going to a fancy dress party in one of the messes, and it was fortunate for me that it turned out to be a British officer - and one with a sense of humour at that.

"I remember him constantly grinning, even when telling me I wasn't doing my job properly. Didn't I realise we were in a state of conflict?

"I stammered out my apologies, and the officer said nothing more, before striding off, still grinning, on his way, in his billowing white burnous. Whew!

"Perhaps he was demob-happy. Perhaps he felt sorry for me. He may even have been mellowed by a drop of the hard stuff. Anyway, I counted my blessings once again. I just wanted to forget that little confrontation.

"By now, my time was coming. I was about to be demobbed, when I was told the commanding officer wanted to see me, and wondered what on earth I had done wrong this time.

"I needn't have worried. The CO was affability itself. To my surprise, he ushered me into a chair, and said, 'Thank you Private Foggitt for your excellent service since you joined the army.' I can't remember what else he said, but he rounded it off by telling me I could collect my rations from the cookhouse, and handed me a ticket for the journey home. After that he shook hands and dismissed me.

"You could have knocked me down with a copy of Part One orders. After all, my army career had not exactly been covered with glory, and I could only think the colonel said the same words to all the men.

"However, a detested sergeant-major, who used to tell us he had been hanging on the wire at Mons before us bastards were born, brought me back to reality. He told me I had probably held up the D-Day landings by six months.

"He knew his men rather better than the CO!"

A mystery which has exercised Bill's mind since his days in Palestine, is whatever became of Private Archie Bick?

"Archie was a likeable person who hailed from Devon. We met up in Tripoli and got on extremely well together, but once I was posted to Palestine, I didn't expect to see him again.

"You can imagine my surprise, therefore, when he suddenly popped up again in Tel Aviv and finished up in the next bed to me. We decided to go out and celebrate, and strayed into a civilian bar, where the barman, a big, greasy-looking fellow, seemed to take great pleasure in serving us with measures of an aniseed-tasting drink.

"That was to prove fatal, as I have learned since. Never touch anything tasting of aniseed in a Middle East bar if you wish to preserve your sanity. At least not unless you are used to the stuff. It seemed so innocuous at first ... but the next thing I knew, I was outside, lying in the road, with my anxious pals all round me.

"'It's only Willy - the poor sod's drunk,' I heard them say. Of Archie there was no sign. He never returned to his bed, and I never saw him again. I still wonder what became of him, and just hope he was all right."

Even when leaving the army, Bill couldn't stay out of trouble.

On the troopship, steaming up the English Channel, which was like Masefield's "mad March day", he was so seasick that he just lay down on the deck, not caring whether or not anyone stepped on him.

"All I can remember is one chap saying, 'What's the matter with this bugger then. Is he dead? He's been here for ages.'"

Thus, somewhat ingloriously, Bill left the armed forces, his part in winning the war not exactly written on tablets of stone; more with a slightly self-conscious gratitude for his deliverance.

"There are some places men are not meant to be, and for me that place was the British army," he admits ruefully.

A Study of Bill in his "deer-stalker" days.

The lady friend who could have changed Bill's life. Cynthia and the weatherman in the grounds of Fountains Abbey, near Ripon.

Bill (in the background) with a much younger Michael Fish (second from the right), in the Lake District following their weather contest. Bill's house-keeper, Betty Cook, is in the foreground.

Bill, dwarfed by the huge mahogany book-case and table in the living room of his home.

In a reflective mood, the sage relaxes by a roaring fire with "Polly".

Back to his roots. Bill takes a look at the "Blue Bell", Egglescliff, Yarm.

Bill outside the parish Church of Thirsk. Bill used to look across from his home to the weather vane (inset) on the church steeple, to see which way the wind was blowing. Because of his failing eyesight he no longer does so.

A lengthy family tree. (left to right): Mrs Tricia Foggitt, Bill, Dr. Paul Foggitt and Mrs Margaret Bird handle the 45-foot long genealogical record with care.

Dr. Paul Foggitt and family tree.

Bill with the aneroid barometer which was a wedding present to his parents in 1912.

Still smiling at 85!

CHAPTER 6

A DOOMED MARRIAGE

On his return from the army, Bill resumed his studies at Lampeter, from where he confidently expected to emerge with a white collar round his neck. He assumed that with his degree, it would only be a matter of time before he emulated his erstwhile colleagues, who had not served with the armed forces, and obtained a living.

But it was not to be. His diaries for the immediate post-war years record a prolonged period of contrasting situations, during which eagerness, optimism and despair walk and in hand, up to his final farewell to the Church of England.

The entries tell of endless meetings involving the college principal, various ministers of the Church, and even the Archbishop of York's representative, as he struggled to find a way round indifferent performances in the General Certificate of Ordination examination.

Bill mourned, "I spent years agonising over my chances of acquiring a living, but eventually realised that I was more at home in the Methodist church. So I said goodbye to the Anglican faith, and went back to being a humble local preacher in what was, after all, my original church.

"However, an even more important reason for my reluctance to fight on, was my desperate need for money, and the only way to overcome this problem was to find a job in the real world.

"My decision involved a lot of heart-searching and self-recrimination, but looking back, I am sure I made the right choice. I honestly do not believe I would have made a good vicar - or Methodist minister, for that matter, although I was much more suited for the latter."

Then Bill revealed why he so badly needed money, and talked about his best-kept "secret".

Although he had mentioned it, years ago, to a local newspaper, only those friends closest to him knew that he was, in fact, married.

"Married?" people will say. "Old Bill, living like a recluse in that great house, is married? Well, well - whatever happened to his wife?"

And therein lies a story. A rather tragic story, in which two innocent people have suffered, because their inexperience outweighed their enthusiasm.

They parted nearly 50 years ago, and only saw each other once since then.

Yet neither ever petitioned for divorce.

Bill's romance with Dora Winifred Kevan, daughter of the Rev A D Kevan, vicar of Kirby Knowle, near Thirsk, began in the 1930s, and continued throughout the war.

They met at a party, and Bill was immediately attracted to the pleasant, smiling clergyman's daughter. They started going out together, and on two or three occasions, Bill would help her father by reading the lesson in church.

His suit, as it were, was not harmed by the fact that in 1939 he was accepted at Lampeter as a trainee priest.

At the beginning of the war, Win, who had trained a s a nurse, joined the Wrens, and the couple agreed to keep in touch by letter. Her father died in 1940 and her mother left the vicarage to live at Borrowby, a village north of Thirsk.

Bill recalled, "I remember her saying to me once, 'If you can bring some happiness into my daughter's life, you will have done more than we could ever do,' and it was then that I realised that she and Win had not had an easy time.

"When we were married, she told me about the domestic difficulties that had existed between her parents."

During their correspondence with each other throughout the war, the couple had discussed marriage at length, and on Easter Tuesday, 1946, shortly after Bill's demob, they walked up the aisle together at St. Mary's church, Bagby, near Thirsk.

The ceremony, which one would have thought merited a euphoric entry in Bill's diary, is recorded, however, in just two bland, unemotional sentences, "Win and I were married at St.. Mary's, Bagby. After the reception at South Villa, we arrived in Chester about 7 pm."

That is all. No words about a radiant bride, champagne toasts, or a confetti send-off.

However, the future looked rosy enough. There were high hopes for Bill, who had returned to Lampeter, and at this stage of his career he had the unswerving support of his wife.

The honeymoon, according to Bill, was a great success. He had come out of the army with a sizeable sum of money, of which a not-inconsiderable proportion was spent gallivanting round excellent hotels, in various resorts, and led to his colleagues at Lampeter wondering whether he was ever coming back.

He said, "We rushed into marriage without a thought for the future. Maybe it was because we had waited for so long, as so many wartime couples did; maybe we were afraid that time would pass us by; it may even have been a reaction against our respective backgrounds. I just don't know."

But even at that early stage, dark clouds were gathering.

The greatest threat to the newly-weds was that they had no home of their own, and became caught up in what must nowadays be an unthinkable concept - a legally married couple living in separate homes.

Win moved into her mother's tiny cottage in Borrowby, while Bill stayed with his parents at South Villa.

The cottage was far too small to accommodate them, while Bill's father had conceived a hearty dislike for Win which made it impossible to think of setting up a domicile there.

So he and his wife "commuted" four miles into their state of matrimony, confused and frustrated.

Bill recalled, "Father was rude and sarcastic towards Win, which made things worse. He would tell me he did not want her under the same roof, and you can imagine how I felt about that."

The situation was little short of farcical, summed up by a typical diary entry, "Win came to tea with us" - as if she were a distant cousin. This was just two months after the wedding.

On August 16th Bill noted "Win rang up in the evening, asking me to spend the night at Borrowby, but I didn't accept." (Why on earth not?) Bill couldn't explain this, but it seemed to leave Win with the high moral ground.

However, the following day the diary recorded, "Had supper with Win, Dick (her brother) and Mrs Kevan."

It was almost unnatural, and it comes as no surprise to find out from the diary on September 15th, 1946, that Win had obtained a post at The Towers nursing home in Saltburn, on Yorkshire's north east coast.

But at least her move had the effect of clearing the air. Bill got on with his studies at Lampeter, and their relationship actually improved. They wrote affectionate letters to each other, and when Bill was home he would pop over to Saltburn, where they spent pleasurable hours walking around local beauty spots. They also did a bit of cycling together.

But his promising career was by now stuttering.

On December 4th he pencilled in his diary, "The Rev John (vicar of Sowerby) said he had heard from the Archbishop that he was not accepting me as an ordinand candidate."

On April 27th, 1947, he received confirmation of the fact that the Archbishop no longer accepted him as an ordinand. Nevertheless he sat his General Certificate of Ordination exams, only to diarise in July, "Hopes of ordination not high after learning GCO results."

By this time Win's patience with her husband's vacillating career prospects had worn thin, and she advised him pointedly that he was wasting his time. He should, she insisted, be considering taking up a career in teaching.

On July 6th he wrote, "Relations between Win and myself deteriorated during the day", and yet on August 9th he was once again saying, "Ordination prospects are clearer, and the wearing of the cloth can now be visualised."

However, on January 9th, 1948, open warfare broke out between them.

The diary recorded "She scorned my position, and accused me of never having worked. Yet I am trying my hardest and have tried my best to please her, always doing my best to fit in with her plans."

In the end, Bill realised that this dreamy state of affairs could go on no longer. Despite the occasional encouraging noise, he knew he was not getting anywhere, and would have to go out into the "real" world to find work.

So it was with a heavy heart that he accepted defeat, and went to see the college principal. "I explained my marital situation, and the fact that, relying on matrimonial grants, I was desperately short of money.

"He was sympathetic, but fully understood, and so I left Lampeter, a sadly disillusioned man. All those years wasted. Dreams turned to ashes."

On the other hand, he was anxious to show Win that he had the drive to look after her. He had never forgotten her mother's sad words, "If you can bring a little happiness into my daughter's life ..."

Bill continued his story, "I managed to obtain a position at a school in Thurnscoe, in the mining area of South Yorkshire, teaching English and the scriptures.

"It was not my ideal choice, but at least I was bringing in an independent wage at last, and felt quite proud of myself. I had also followed Win's exhortation to get a teaching job."

But educating miners' sons was not like teaching choirboys, although admittedly even they can present problems. Bill's pupils were tough, boisterous and irreverent, and it wasn't long before his diary once again told a tale of misery and uncertainty.

As a religious teacher he could hardly go round bashing ears to gain attention, and, of course, his mildness was construed as weakness.

His mind went back to those earthy days. "The boys were rough because, living in a mining community, that was the only life they knew. Their fathers had dangerous jobs, and they themselves anticipated following them underground, so naturally they had no time for fancy etiquette or flowery phrases. They called a spade a bloody great shovel, and that was that.

"There was seldom any malice in them. Anything they had to say, they said it to your face. And they didn't lack a sense of humour either. I once tapped a boy on the head, and he promptly dropped to the classroom floor, feigning unconsciousness.

"'You've killed him, sir,' yelled his pals. 'Yes', agreed the 'victim', - 'you've killed me sir!' I had to laugh.

"Now I was assured that the following tale was not apocryphal. Apparently one lad had gone home and told his parents he was illiterate. 'What?' roared his father. 'We'll soon settle that. First thing in the morning we'll be there with your birth certificate.' The other masters swore this was true.

"I once took a party of boys on a nature walk - something I was well-equipped to do - and pointed out a clump of hawkweed, which I told them was at one time used by poor people as 'tobacco'.

"Later I noticed that one lad was missing, and became rather worried. I needn't have done, because suddenly the youngster reappeared with his arms full of the weed. He explained that he was going to turn it into tobacco."

However, one day, boisterous good humour gave way to naked violence.

The smile left Bill's features as he recalled a small, bespectacled master called Flanagan, a mild man who would not - and probably could not - hurt a fly, who had chastised a boy for being unruly.

The following day the lad's father, a burly miner, appeared in the classroom.

"Is thy name Flanagan?" he asked the unsuspecting teacher, who replied that he was. "Well, this is for chastising my lad," replied the neanderthal, and without any warning landed a haymaker of a punch which sent poor Flanagan flying into a cupboard.

His glasses shattered, and he lay dazed.

With that the father turned on his heel and left. Said Bill, "I don't know whether any further action was taken, but I suspect it wasn't.

"That did it for me. We obviously needed danger money to teach properly in those parts, and I decided to get out while I was in one piece. The headmaster, in the kindest possible way, told me I wasn't cut out for teaching, although he tried to persuade me to stay on. All I needed, he added, was a lot of patience.

"I could have replied that a suit of armour would be quite useful as well."

Time has, however, a way of mellowing the worst memories. Bill remembers one day when racing was taking place in Thirsk, being accosted by two smartly-dressed young men. "It's Mr Foggitt, isn't it?" one of them said. "You won't remember us, but you used to teach us in Thurnscoe."

"Those thick South Yorkshire accents said it all, and I must say I was delighted to be recognised. We had quite a long chat before they went off to back horses, and knowing something of the South Yorkshire mentality, I thought they wouldn't be unduly worried about whether they won or lost - just as long as they had a good day out."

Bill's next appointment was at a much bigger and more sophisticated school in Stoke-on-Trent. It proved to be an uneventful part of his career, and he managed two years before he realised that his former headmaster had been right. He just wasn't cut out for teaching, so he left and eventually took a job as a humble storeman with ICI in Birmingham. It was about this time that matters between Win and him came to a head. "In fairness to her, she said her position was with me, and actually came down to look at the digs where I was staying.

"She had her little black dog with her, from whom she was inseparable, so you can imagine her chagrin when, having travelled all that way, the landlady flew into a tizzy and said there was no way she was having any animals in her home.

"That was the end of any thought of Win coming to stay with me. She promptly turned round and left for home.

"One day I found her sobbing. She had been talking to her brother, she told me, and he had suggested it was time we parted, and she agreed. He was right, of course. The marriage had been stuttering along for too long, and we had, quite simply, fallen out of love.

"Nevertheless, it still came as a blow, although in a way I was also relieved.

"Afterwards, people told me it was the best thing that could have happened.

"Win was a bit of a snob and thought she was above me socially. She would belittle me in front of other people, and could be very moody. While I could sympathise with her for disliking my father, I couldn't understand why she criticised my mother, who was the soul of kindness towards her.

"Despite this, however, she was a nice girl and deserved better than me. I still feel mildly guilty about not giving her the things she wanted; children, for example. I couldn't help thinking about the unhappy life she had lived, and her mother's appeal to me when we were going out together.

"I recalled her outpouring of grief when she returned home one day to find her mother lying on the floor, having suffered a stroke. In her hand she was clutching a note from her son, apparently telling her he had separated from his wife. She died soon afterwards.

"I thought of Win's anguish when her little dog died.

"I thought about the children she'd wanted, but never had, and I remembered the words of a song she used to sing sadly, 'There is nothing left for me ... '

"And I knew that I had failed again." Bill later found out that Win was living in Cumbria, but she died last year and the funeral service was held at her father's former church at Kirby Knowle, near Thirsk.

The vicar, the Rev. Toddy Hoare, persuaded Bill to attend the service, but he commented afterwards. "It was completely unreal to me. Win's brother was very nice, but I don't really know what I was doing there. I had no feelings for Win, and I confess I grieved more for my little dog, Polly, who died about the same time."

CHAPTER 7

THE CONCRETE JUNGLE

E ngland's second city absorbed the credulous countryman with the contempt that all large conurbations reserve for those who tread timidly through their concrete canyons.

Bill was simply swallowed up by the industrial monolith, to become an anonymous cog among its million moving parts.

For 15 years he lived in a series of flats and bedsits; never having enough money because of his lack of qualifications; discovering that violence was just round the corner, or trying to come to terms with carousing Irishmen or West Indians every weekend.

He experienced the brutality of city life at first hand - a great shock to his country culture - which was brought home to him when he was awakened in the middle of the night, to witness a crowd of blacks underneath his window, fighting furiously. "I kept my head down, you can be sure."

On another occasion he heard a screaming, and looked out through his window to see a black man holding a knife to a woman's throat. Even Bill knew the dangers of interfering between protagonists, and quietly returned to bed. "The pavement was unstained by blood the following morning," he said, "so I assumed that the drama did not reach Shakespearean proportions."

Then there was the night when all hell broke loose. Once again a mob of West Indians went on the rampage in the street where Bill lived. He said there was one terrible night when fighting was abruptly brought to a halt by an explosion.

Someone had apparently thrown a home-made bomb. Said Bill, "This was really serious. The walls of the digs shook, and it was sufficient to break up the melee.

"This was on a Saturday night, and when I attended chapel the following morning someone said to me, 'We're so relieved to see you, Bill. We heard about the disturbance and thought you might have been killed. How on earth do you live where you do?'

"I told her, 'distinctively uncomfortably.'"

But trouble didn't always stop outside Bill's flat. One night, he was reading as peacefully as he could under the circumstances, when, without warning, a smartly-dressed, but hysterical woman burst into his room. Said Bill, "She gasped out that she was in terrible trouble. Her husband was after her, armed with a knife, and was going to kill her. Could I possibly lend her some money to get to Worcester?

"As usual, when confronted by the unexpected, I froze. Then it came to me that if her husband really was on the warpath, the last thing I wanted was for him to find her in my flat.

"To my mind she was simply a woman in distress, and I was anxious to help.

"But a loan? That seemed to be a bit of a laugh. To an hysterical woman in a dingy street, in a city of a million people?

"She told me she would repay it the following week. I didn't have a lot of money, but handed over as much as she needed, and she departed, swearing undying thanks. I seem to remember she said she was related to the Bishop of Worcester, and I thought, yes, and I'm the Archbishop of Canterbury.

"My flatmate told me I'd seen the last of my money, but lo and behold, some days later there was a knock on my door, and there she stood, composed and smiling, with my money in her hand.

"'I've come to repay my debt,' she said. 'I'm so sorry for barging in on you the other night, and hope you'll forgive me.' Then with profuse thanks, she left, without further explanation.

"Now in a huge, anonymous place like Birmingham, I wonder what the odds against someone turning up like that must be. She made no reference to the incident which led to the request in the first place, and I didn't ask her, but for a while it certainly lifted my spirits, as well as faith in human nature."

Bill also had to get used to the "Brummie" sense of humour. One day he excitedly told his foreman at the ICI factory where he had obtained a job as a storeman, "There's a placard outside. It says Stalin's dead," to which his phlegmatic superior rejoined, "So's Queen Anne, and I'm not feeling too good miself."

After delivering his earth-shaking piece of news, Bill felt severely deflated.

News that would set a small town like Thirsk alight, was accepted as a matter of indifference in the city. Stalin, the bloodthirsty dictator, had died - so what?

But life in the city took a more dramatic turn on the night Bill found himself confronted by cold steel.

It happened one evening when he was having a cup of coffee in New Street station buffet, chatting to a casual acquaintance. Then the general hum of conversation was interrupted.

81

"Suddenly the door crashed open, and in lurched a burly Irishman, obviously the worse for drink. I had always got on well with Paddies who lived in my area, but unfortunately my companion and I made the mistake of sniggering, and that was a terrible mistake.

"What is it about drunks, despite their stupefied condition, that makes them so acutely aware of what they consider to be a slight?"

"All I know was that he was suddenly towering over use, weaving about, and waving a vicious-looking knife a few inches from my face. The laughter stopped. 'You bloody Brummies are taking the Mickey,' he snarled. 'I'll teach you to poke fun at me.'

"My gallant city acquaintance had, by this time, done a vanishing act, probably escaping under the table, leaving me to face the angry Celt. "I stammered that I wasn't a Brummie and hadn't intended to cause any offence. To my surprise, he lowered the knife.

"'So ye're not a Brummie eh? And where would ye be from? I explained that I was from Yorkshire, and to my continuing surprise he slurred, 'From Yorkshire? Well in that case I'll be apologising. It's just that I hate these bloody Brummies. Do ye know Catterick?'

"I told him the camp was a few miles from where I lived, and he said his brother was stationed there. What a meeting of minds! Then this huge chap with hands like shovels, who a few seconds before had been going to stick a knife in me, grinned affably and offered to buy me a cup of tea.

"However, I decided I had been lucky thus far, and knowing how quickly drunks can change their moods, made an excuse and left, his inebriated farewells echoing behind me."

Bill's knowledge of the opposite sex was still not very advanced, despite his marriage. He took females at face value, never suspecting anything so unsporting as subterfuge.

So it was that he was standing at a bus stop in pouring rain one evening after finishing work, when a young woman came up to him with tears in her eyes. She told him she needed to catch the bus, but hadn't any money to pay the fare. She explained that she had parted from her husband.

Of course, Bill couldn't see a damsel in distress, so without any hesitation he said he would pay the fare, and they boarded the bus together.

Bill took up the story. "When we got to where she wanted to get off, she asked me if I would like to go to her home for a cup of coffee, and to dry my clothes. Foolishly I agreed.

"We made our way to a terraced home, and she went straight into the kitchen, telling me to make myself comfortable in the living room.

"I sank gratefully into an armchair, anticipating a cup of hot coffee, when, without any waning, the door burst open, and I found myself looking into the bloodshot eyes of a very large man who had obviously been drinking.

"Behind him was a smaller man with grey hair.

"The big man was in a savage mood. 'Who the hell are you, and what are you doing with my wife,' he roared. And with that he grabbed me by the lapels and lifted me bodily out of the chair, before flinging me back again.

"I was completely confused and tried to stammer out why I was there; that I hadn't any idea the lady was married, and had merely helped her out with her bus fare. (Which I seem to remember was about four pence.)

"But he wouldn't listen, explaining in graphic language what he was going to do to me. He told me to stay in the chair, and I was too frightened to move.

"Then, to my relief, he seemed to collapse into another chair, and started snoring almost at once, The older man was still there (I thing he must have been the father of one of them), and this is where I'm sure luck came to my rescue, because he noticed a copy of the Methodist Recorder sticking out of my coat pocket, and that must have satisfied him of my honourable intentions and that I was anything but a fly-by-night gigolo.

"He told me not to worry - everything would be all right. I would just have to let him sleep it off, but I had better stay put, because the big man might suddenly awaken. "And the woman? She never reappeared. I don't know what became of her. I don't know whether she was married, separated or single, and to the best of my recollection the men didn't explain either. It was - and is - a complete mystery to me.

"Anyway, the giant eventually came round. He became quite amiable and accepted my explanation of what had happened. In fact he went even further, and ran me home in his car, although I don't know how far he would have got in these days of breath-testing."

One house Bill stayed at had been converted into flats, mainly occupied by Irish labourers. He couldn't stop chuckling as he remembered their antics.

"They were a cheerful, good-humoured lot, but used to get plenty to drink at weekends and liked to carouse. However, they were always considerate to me, and I liked them a lot.

"But one thing puzzled me. Why was it that a Roman Catholic priest turned up on the doorstep every Monday morning?

"It transpired that he was usually enquiring about why certain members of his flock had not been at mass the previous day. One such was Paddy Murphy. The Irish lads were constantly making excuses for him.

"He had been visiting relatives ... he was looking for a new job ... he was ill ... anything to satisfy the man of God.

"But he was tenacious and kept calling round, and the Paddies were running out of excuses.

"However, they had one more shot in their locker. The father arrived as usual on Monday, and would they kindly tell him where Paddy Murphy was. They told him they didn't know, but his holiness was welcome to come in and see for himself.

"Eventually the priest left, nonplussed. But I knew where Paddy Murphy was.

"He was hiding underneath my bed - a moral coward in the face of the Church. 'Jaysus, but that was close,' he muttered as he crawled out.

"I have often wondered about those Irishmen. They would - in drink at least - face a charging rhinoceros, yet were terrified of the priest. Mind you, they were probably even more horrified about foregoing a weekend's boozing, which of course, was the reason why so many of them missed mass on Sunday morning."

There was a time when Bill fervently began to wish he was more worldly-wise.

It was Friday, and they had just been paid. Bill went to the washroom to tidy up, and trustingly put his wage packet on the side until he had finished his ablutions.

When he turned round, it had vanished. He was facing a weekend without any money and without any food in his flat. He knew who the thief was, but couldn't prove it.

In despair he did what any sensible Englishman would have done. He went to the nearest police station to report the theft, but more importantly, to see if he could borrow some money to tide him over the weekend.

"It was a bit cheeky, I suppose, but I had no food in and was desperate.

"I remember being ushered in front of an imposing looking officer with thimbles on his shoulders.

"He looked very stern, and after I'd explained the situation, asked me where I was from. I told him I was from Yorkshire, and he seemed to relax a little. 'Well,' he replied, 'I've never been let down by a Yorkshireman yet.' And with that, he reached into a pocket and pulled out a £5 note. 'That should keep you going,' he added.

"However, trust only goes so far, and he took the precaution of giving me a lift back to my digs. And who could blame him?

"Anyway, it was a nice gesture, and the police went up considerably in my estimation. Needless to say I went round the following weekend to pay my debt. The inspector warned me about being too trusting, and I still feel bitter about a man who could so blatantly rob a workmate."

A tale Bill takes great delight in telling, concerns the time he "disappeared" before the very faces of a congregation, while conducting a service in a Birmingham Methodist church.

"To this day I don't know how it happened, but instead of mounting the pulpit steps, I found myself in a corridor which led to the organ loft, I stumbled along in the gloom, and suddenly I was looking down at the organist through a glass panel. At the same instant he happened to glance up - to see my bewildered face.

"He looked absolutely terrified, and it looked for a moment as if he was going to make a run for if. His hands froze on the keys, and the music ground to a fitful halt.

"I hastily retraced my steps, and this time managed to find my way to the pulpit. I was relieved, and the congregation appeared equally relieved to realise that I was not a wizard, after all.

"But I think it took the organist a little longer to recover from his 'visitation from on high.'"

During his time in Birmingham, Bill found himself with plenty of spare time, and became a regular visitor to the Magistrates and Assize courts. "I found it fascinating to see justice in action," he recalled, "but I couldn't repress a shudder when, on three occasions, I watched the judge don the black cap, which meant that murderers were to be hanged."

Bill had been in Birmingham for about three years, when he had the good fortune to meet Cynthia, a smartly-dressed, well-spoken divorcee, with whom he was to find love and companionship for the next decade.

They met through the Methodist church, and immediately "hit it off".

Cynthia was everything Bill had ever imagined a woman should be. Attractive and humorous, but practical and shrewd. She also had a four-year-old son.

Whereas his early love for Audrey had been built round a dream, Cynthia was of the real world, and as time went by, Bill came to cherish their relationship. She was like a rock in his rather confused and tangled existence.

They went everywhere together. To church; to cafes; to the cinema, and to the park. They would often take Robert, her son, with them - sometimes, occasionally, to church when Bill was preaching.

They would also go to Cynthia's mother's home for tea.

Bill once pawned his wrist watch to pay for their seats at a picture house, and when they visited the park, would enthusiastically kick a ball about with Robert.

Said Bill, "When I met Cynthia I was a lonely young man, going nowhere. She came into my empty life and gave me love, and, as you can imagine, this gave me an infinitely greater sense of security.

"How can I every forget the sheer joy of returning to New Street station, after visiting my parents, to see her there, waiting to greet me with a smile and a hug. It was like coming home, and lit up even the wretched surroundings of Birmingham.

"I am sure Cynthia loved me, and would have married me, had I asked."

But Bill didn't pop the question. Getting a divorce from Win would, presumably, have proved easy enough, but there were other things on his mind.

He had no job prospects other than waiting for "Buggins' turn", and lacked the confidence to take on the responsibility of looking after Cynthia and her son.

"I was very poorly paid, and felt hopelessly inadequate. Looking back, I realise I should have grasped the nettle and taken my chances while they were there. Cynthia had told me several times about how difficult it was, bringing up a son without a father, and that should have been my cue. A more mature man would have seen the significance of her remarks.

"I suppose, too, I was taking Cynthia for granted. After all, we seemed to be very happy as we were. I should have seen the warning signs ... our meetings gradually became fewer, and finally stopped. I remember one particular row. Cynthia's mother was away for the weekend and playfully I remarked, 'At last, peace, perfect peace.' Normally Cynthia would laughed this off, but not this time. She fixed me with a cold stare, and replied, 'You really meant that, didn't you? I knew then that something had gone wrong between us, and some months later I received a letter from her saying she had become engaged to another man.

"The news hit me like a bombshell. My life seemed to fall apart, and I cursed my indecision. I couldn't sleep at nights, and when I did, I would wake up, crying out to God to bring her back to me.

"But God didn't, preferring to help those who help themselves.

"Once again my life was empty. I wandered aimlessly about the streets. I went into Birmingham cathedral and prayed for her return. I retraced our lovely walks, and was particularly sad when I went to a lovely little chapel we had attended, and saw our names, side by side, in the visitors' book.

"When I arrived back at New Street station, after visiting Thirsk, I half expected to see Cynthia waiting there, just as before. The sense of emptiness I experienced was appalling, but I had only myself to blame.

"Anyway, Cynthia re-married and went away from Birmingham, but tragically, her new husband died not long afterwards, and she now lives on the Isle of Wight.

"To my great joy, we are in touch again, and occasionally write to each other. Sometimes Cynthia will phone me, and I find it lovely to chat to her. I even went once to the Isle of Wight to stay and found it a lovely place.

"I believe, at one time, she may have wanted me to go the island, which is a delightful place to live, but I could not bring myself to leave Yorkshire again."

And so, on that rather sad note, Bill finally realised that not even the lure of "wonderful Cynthia" could lure him away from South Villa, and the hills and green meadows of his native county.

During his 17 years in the midlands, following his failure as a teacher in Hanley, Stoke-on-Trent, the extent to which the "country boy's" inexperience, lack of qualifications, and lack of knowledge about mathematics held him back can be gleaned from his employment record, involving at least 12 jobs, most of them lasting for only a couple of months or so.

This was his record: Birmingham city valuer's office; a clerical position with the Birmingham Mail; clerical employment with a butcher and slaughterer; selling weighing machines; storeman; application for position of prison officer at Winson Green, turned down, not surprisingly by the governor who felt his temperament was not suited to the job; storeman in the ammunition depot at ICI; job with a firm of printers; clerk at Aston railway goods depot; employment with a paper and printing works (which lasted for a lengthy 18 months), and finally an amazing three/four years with C.B. Frost, manufacturers of rubber goods.

As this record shows, his life became a series of disruptions, during which he often reached the point of desperation. He became used to having only a couple of shillings in his pocket, and on several occasions had to borrow money to survive.

His only relief came from small amounts his mother was able to send him.

His received no support from his father, whose hard-hearted attitude towards his shortcomings could so easily have been replaced by a sympathetic understanding of his predilection for literature or the ministry.

One can now understand why he was so reticent about proposing to Cynthia.

Bill's wife , Dora Winifred, pictured in the grounds of Kirby Knowle vicarage in happier times.

The wedding that was almost unrecorded in Bill's diary. A family photograph showing Bill and Win (front row, third and fourth from right).

Bill's mother, Mrs Elizabeth Foggitt (front), on the occasion of her 90th birthday in 1971. Back row (left to right): Bill's niece, Bill, Bill's sister, Betty Anne.

If it's seaweed it must mean rain

COME rain or shine, our weather never ceases to fascinate.

And it has fascinated Bill Foggitt for most of his 79 years.

Now Bill, veteran of scores of television and newspaper forecasts, has produced a book in which he opens a treasure-chest of weather fact, fiction and folklore.

Not for him the satellites, computers and massive back-up team the Michael Fishes, Suzanne Charltons and Alex Hills of TV depend upon for their forecasts.

For the predictions that have made him famous, Britain's top amateur weather-watcher would rather rely on a few observations of his own . . .

Such as the erratic behaviour of Blackie, his cat. That, Bill says, is a sure sign that windy weather is on the way.

Or the pine cone hanging by his door.

He checks it each morning to see whether it is going to rain.

Seaweed, frogspawn, flies, spiders, squirrels, sheep – phenomena as unlikely as the weather itself – all help give Bill an insight into what lies ahead.

The Foggitt family have been monitoring the weather in Thirsk, North Yorkshire, since 1881. Bill took over the

RAIN CHECK: Bill relies on his seaweed

By SIMON FERRARI

job 25 years ago. Among the weird and wacky weather facts he has accumulated over the years:

● IN the severe winter of 1814 the Thames froze over for nine weeks.

The ice was so thick that an elephant was able to walk down it – and did.

● THE world's coldest place is Vostok in Antarctica with an average annual temperature of minus 57.8 deg C.

● THE driest place on earth is the Desierto de Atacama in Chile.

It did rain there in 1971 . . . for the first time in about 400 years.

So much for Britain's drought!

Weatherwise by Bill Foggitt. Published by Pavilion Books at £4.99.

National fame - a selection of the many headlines from the daily newspapers.

Wintry words of Bill the sage

BATTEN down the hatches and turn up the central heating because winter is about to get cold . . . very cold. So says BILL FOGGIT, the controversial weather forecaster and author, who has meteorological records dating back 150 years. Here Bill explains why he thinks we are in for a big freeze.

I MAKE long-term weather forecasts from studying the daily weather records kept by my father, grandfather and great-grandfather.

My own diaries, kept since I was a schoolboy in the Twenties, also play their part.

After comparing the weather of the summer and autumn of 1976 with 1995, I have a very good idea of the kind of winter we are about to have.

November 1976 was comparatively mild but early in December I recorded in my diary that the birds were stripping the holly berries from the trees — building up reserves for severe conditions.

Early that month, I recorded a sharp fall in both night and day temperatures, bringing the mean temperature for December 1976 down to 35F, which is five degrees below average, in one of the coldest Decembers on our records this century.

My own records show that the weather for the second half of 1976 and 1995 was almost identical — June 1976 brought only a quarter of an inch of rain, while June 1995 brought three quarters of an inch (average rainfall for June for this century is 1.97 inches).

July 1976 recorded 1.54 inches of

LIFELONG STUDY: Bill Foggit

rain below average, August 0.4 of an inch. It was one of the driest summers on record, followed by the next very hot dry summer of 1995.

We get a very hot, dry summer every 20 years or so as in 1955, 1933, 1911, 1895 and, of course, 1976 and 1995. They are always followed by severe frosts.

Studying this 20-year cycle of long, hot, dry summers, I notice that at such times sunspot activity is at its minimum.

These areas of disturbance on the sun's surface cause violent gales and well above average rainfall.

The lack of disturbance in the atmosphere contributes to cold climatic conditions. In 1976, there were 190 days where no sunspot activity was recorded.

Studying nature also provides clues to weather patterns.

One old saying goes: "When squirrels early start to hoard, winter will pierce us like a sword."

In the woodlands around my home in Thirsk, North Yorkshire, the squirrels have been hastily gathering nuts in preparation for a long, hard winter.

They hoarded early last year and I recorded one of the most severe Februaries of this century.

On top of this, a farmer friend informed me a few weeks ago that the swallows and martins, which generally arrive in April and leave in early October, left this year in mid-September — another sign of a long and very hard winter ahead.

● The Met Office is dubious about Mr Foggit's methods. "We have given up trying to judge the winter to come by comparing past summers." says press officer Malcolm Brooks. "Hot summers have been followed by all sorts of winters."

BILL FOGGIT's books: Weatherwise (published by Pavilion, £4.99) and The Yorkshire Weather Book (Countryside Books, £6.95).

91

CHAPTER 8

A PAINFUL INTRODUCTION
TO A NEW CAREER

Bill returned home in 1966 and immediately started looking for a suitable job. However, he soon found that positions were not as easy to come by as in bustling Birmingham, and once again depression was beginning to settle on him, when fate stepped in - albeit extremely - and pointed the way to the skies.

He was returning from York during a violent thunderstorm, and the bus obligingly stopped near his home. Intent only on getting under cover, Bill dashed out - straight into the path of an oncoming car, which was unable to avoid him.

He was rushed to hospital with a badly smashed right leg. For the next three months surgeons fought to save the limb, and eventually succeeded, but only after six operations, including two bone grafts and numerous blood transfusions. When he left hospital the surgeon said, "Now Bill, I want you to do two things: get plenty of walking in and drink two pints of beer a day." Said Bill with a deep sense of satisfaction, "I have taken both pieces of advice very seriously."

Then he was sent home to recuperate and ponder his future, but, armed with only his theological degree, his prospects were as cheerless as an east coast sea fret.

And then one day, as she watched her son hobbling aimlessly about the house, his mother had a bright idea. An idea that was to make the following three decades the happiest of his life.

Why not copy out the weather records, which had been compiled by his forebears on individual sheets of paper, and which lay gathering dust in the mahogany bookcase?

Mrs Foggitt's therapeutic suggestion struck an instant chord with Bill. He was aware of the records, but did not appreciate the vast amount of information they contained.

The marathon exercise he now undertook would have deterred Dickens' Bob Cratchitt, but how rewarding it turned out to be.

Thousands of meticulously recorded facts and figures pertaining to climactic behaviour, stretching back over a century, rolled off his pen, providing a meteorological umbilical cord between the past and present.

The archives contained details of tempests, such as the one which swept the Tay railway bridge to destruction in 1879; disastrous floods, droughts and memorable heatwaves, which engrossed Bill to such an extent that he hardly realised the pain in his leg was receding.

He was particularly interested in the weather cycles his predecessors had pinpointed, and in due course satisfied himself through his own observations, that these really did occur over a succession of years.

Generally, these cycles covered three-year periods (with occasional aberrations), during which heavy rain on two successive years would be followed by warm, dry conditions on the third,and vice versa.

Two typical examples, plucked from the records, were the extremely wet summers of 1930 and 1931, which were followed by an absolute scorcher in 1933; and the winters of 1962 and 1963, which were intensely cold, while that of 1964 was surprisingly mild.

So often had this formula held true during the period of the records, that Bill came to place implicit trust in it when asked for long range forecasts.

His simple explanation is that nature is balancing itself out, particularly when extremes of weather occur, such as the summer of 1976, when a record drought was followed by record rainfall in September.

He realises, of course, that this pattern is often subject to variations, such as happens when sunspot activity is at its height, and it was this that caught him out in the summer of 1998, when his prediction of fine, dry weather was blown sky high, and Britain fumed at its worst summer season for years.

Yes, Bill has often got it wrong; he has never claimed to be infallible, but he consoles himself with the knowledge that his evaluation of the weather has more often than not been correct.

The only time he lost his cool with a critic, was when a malicious fault-finder kept ringing him up and abusing him, and in the end he was obliged to call in the police.

In defence of his balancing theory, he trawled back through his records, and discovered that, come drought or deluge, rainfall in Thirsk averaged 26.79 inches. In his "Weather Book" of 1978 he gave the figures for the previous ten years: 1968 (27.51);1969 (30.21); 1970 (21.94); 1971 (20.70); 1972 (22.07); 1973 (18.28); 1974 (25.93); 1975 (20); 1976 (26.14); 1977 (22.92).

He said it was also remarkable how little average temperatures varied from year to year. In Thirsk the average was 49 degrees Fahrenheit, taken over a ten-year period as follows: 1968 (46.6); 1969 (47.5); 1970 (46.4); 1971 (49.5); 1972 (48.7); 1973 (49.3); 1974 (49); 1975 (49.4); 1976 (51.6); 1977 (48).

"In the end," he says, "everything balances out - even my bank account."

He has also deduced, again by researching the archives, that really hard winters can be expected every 12 to 15 years, while from his father he learned that sunspot activity, generating gigantic magnetic storms on the sun's surface, peaks approximately every 11 years, sending summer temperatures soaring up, but also leading to thunderstorms and generally unsettled weather.

When this solar activity dies down, Bill maintains that warm - but not too hot - and dry summers can be expected, while in winter, calm spells, resulting in lengthy periods of frost, are more likely to be experienced than blizzards.

He remembers his father, many years ago, regularly peering at the sun through a piece of smoked glass, and explaining to him how sunspots affected our weather. "He warned me never to study it with the naked eye, and preferably in the morning or evening when it wasn't so bright.

"He told me that sunspots were associated with huge magnetic storms, and solar flares, which disrupted weather patterns, and in the ensuing years, through my own observations, I have discovered that this is the case."

The atmospheric turmoil that often - but not always - results from solar eruptions hurling clouds of plasma into the universe at two million miles an hour, can play havoc with meteorological forecasts, and present insurmountable problems for Bill, who has no sophisticated equipment to correct his predictions at short notice.

Solar activity also presents a threat to earth's communication systems, and although satellites can be sent into orbit to detect magnetic disturbances likely to affect our planet, these can also confuse their own computer systems, sending them off course, and thus nullifying their objective.

On the credit side, however, the charged ions bombarding earth are responsible for wonderful auroral displays, such as the one witnessed by Bill at Biggleswade in 1938.

In 1998, there were reports of a huge "sunquake", presumably similar to a sunspot, and the weather that followed was simply appalling, with the exception of a brief heatwave in the southern half of the country. In the north, high winds meant that practically no two consecutive days were alike, and summer was, to all intents and purposes, non-existent.

This was calamitous for Bill, for according to him it should have been fine and warm throughout June, July and August. Instead, it rained and rained ... and only August redeemed his forecast to some extent.

He also relied to some extent on global warming, but such was this British summer that even this was relegated to the back burner.

Bill came in for some stinging criticism from a supermarket chain which paid him £250 to predict these three months for its customers, and he was suitably chastened by the management's indignation.

But in fairness, could anyone have foretold such unpredictable weather, when even the experts regularly got it wrong?

Well, perhaps Piers Corbyn, of Weather Action, could have done so. But then he has specialised in studying sunspot activity, and is well aware of its implications. In fact, he was shrewd enough in 1997 to float his company on the Stock Exchange, based on his knowledge, and was estimated to have made a fortune.

The Met men and women might well be advised to do the same amount of research into the nuclear activity of our star, whose "hiccupping" over the past few billion years might be deemed as responsible for our freakish weather as the volcano, Mount St. Helen's, or the Pacific phenomenon of El Nino.

As I have pointed out, Bill has ever lacked an understanding of money, and his contentment with the status quo has prevented him cashing in on his knowledge as others would have done.

With the help of an agent, maybe he could have become a wealthy man. South Villa could have been restored, and central heating installed, to augment his small fire.

But Bill has never given this a thought. That venerable gentleman remains completely unperturbed by thoughts of pennies from heaven, and is at peace with himself.

For a long time after he switched careers, his long range forecasts were least the equal, and sometimes better, than those of the professionals, who did not have the benefit of his superb records. However, they have redressed the balance with their multi-billion pounds' worth of equipment, situated in all parts of the world.

An example of Bill's pre-eminence in this field was furnished in 1968 when he was asked by a newspaper to predict what sort of a winter it was going to be.

He delved into the records, and told the paper's readers, "Long range weather forecasting is, of course, a dicey business, but there are certain signs that the winter of 1968/9 will be comparatively mild, dry and foggy. Our family records show that a wet summer and mild autumn are invariably followed by rather foggy weather, particularly in December and January."

Bill then launched into his astonishing forecast, almost week by week, which I doubt even the most experienced weathermen would have put their names to.

The article went on, "Already the wet summer and exceptionally warm October have brought dense fogs to the north of England, and these are certain to return ..."

He also referred to his weather allies, the swallows. "Country lore affirms that the longer they stay with use, the shorter the winter, and as these departed on October 4th in this district, it appears to be another good omen.

"It seems we can expect reasonably mild weather during the first week of November, with considerable sunny spells, but a return of the fog towards the middle and end of the month.

"The fogs are likely to return about the middle of December, and will most likely be dense for several successive days.

"Christmas is likely to be cold and damp, with strong, gale force winds, during the last few days of the month, accompanied by a marked drop in temperature, with the probability of snow and sleet.

"The first week of January is likely to be fairly mild and quite sunny, but with quite keen frosts and showers of snow and sleet during the middle of the month."

"But," he warned, "the most intense spells of winter invariably occur during the second week of February, which coincides with Buchan's First Cold Spell of the year, and which brought temperatures in Thirsk down to zero on the nights of the 8th and 10th in 1895."

(Alexander Buchan was a celebrated Scottish meteorologist (1829-1907) who postulated his "spells" theory that the British climate was subject to successive hot and cold spells between certain dates each year.)

Although Mistress Weather didn't always dance to Bill's tune that winter, his diaries show how basically accurate the picture he presented proved to be.

His "considerable sunny spells" turned out to cover only a couple of days, but more significantly fog began to form on the 6th, 10th and 11th, and by the third week it had turned milder.

Incidentally, the Met Office forecast snow for the 15th. Bill disagreed, and the day turned out cloudy and fine. His diary expressed his pleasure at beating the experts.

The following days were misty and mild, and in some areas the fog was dense.

The rest of November was mild and on the 25th the temperature reached 54 degrees.

On the 28th, Bill recorded, "Thirty counties in Britain blanketed by fog."

December mists started a week earlier than predicted, occurring on the 3rd, 4th and 5th, but Bill's forecast was authenticated when they returned on the 10th, 11th and 12th.

Snow and sleet showers on the 14th, 15th, and 16th looked like upsetting the timetable, but mild weather set in on the 18th and lasted until the 23rd.

Christmas Day, sunny and cold, mocked his "cold and damp" prediction, but he was out by only a couple of days, and his forecast for the end of the month was borne out with a vengeance when gale force winds brought snow, which piled up into eight-foot drifts on the nearby Cleveland Hills.

The New Year dawned with considerable sunshine, just as Bill had said it would, and lasted throughout January, without, however, the snow and sleet showers he had predicted, but his prophecy of a generally mild winter was holding up.

And then, just as he had warned, on the eve of the second week in February, the "most intense spell of winter" arrived. Temperatures plummeted, and during the following fortnight Bill's thermometer included the following readings: February 8th, 12 degrees of frost; 9th, 16 degrees; 10th, 11 degrees; 13th, blizzards; 14th, 12 degrees; 15th, 10 degrees; 16th, 16 degrees; 17th, 12 degrees, and 18th, 13 degrees.

The cold spell went on until March.

Anyone seeking a winter forecast would undoubtedly have been delighted with this feat, taking little notice of the occasional overlap or aberration. It certainly was a remarkable achievement, and shows just why the family records have contributed so much to British climatological studies.

Unfortunately, owing to their age and long usage, they are becoming rather untidy, partly because of Bill's failing eyesight, and several have "disappeared". Dr Foggitt has tried his best to put themin order, but said there were "great gaps in this priceless record."

But back to sunspots for a moment.

It was in April 1985 that the now defunct Today newspaper organised a friendly contest between Michael Fish, the BBC's head forecaster, Piers Corbyn, and the gifted amateur from Thirsk, who had just been propelled to fame as a result of his rebuttal of an official Met Office forecast that an Arctic spell would continue.

The three were challenged to predict the weather for July and August, and it was Bill who came out on top with 88 per cent. Corbyn ran him close with 80 per cent, and Fish trailed in third with 74 per cent.

Of course, one swallow doesn't make a summer, and there were other contests which the experts won, although Bill acquitted himself honourably.

However, this was a tangible triumph for the seer from South Villa. "No Drought About It - Bill's The Clear Winner" trumpeted the headline, leaving him with a huge sense of satisfaction.

Later, he explained that his success was a combination of his records, and the fact that he had out-Corbynned Corbyn by correctly interpreting sunspot activity, although on this score he admitted, "I just stuck my neck out."

At any rate, it brought him celebratory drinks from his "magic circle."

Bill had another tussle with Michael Fish, which took place over several days, and this time the BBC man carried the day, although not by a wide margin.

Bill and his housekeeper, Betty Cook, subsequently had lunch with Fish in the Lake District, and a national newspaper pictured the two weathermen having a donkey race on Blackpool sands, although Bill chuckled, "It was a bit of a farce, really. I don't think we got very far, probably a few yards, but I suppose it illustrated the point that Michael and I were in competition."

Although he relies on his records for long range predictions, in his day-to-day life round Thirsk, he is essentially a localised diviner, which particularly applied during the years he was appearing on Yorkshire Television. True - he has come up trumps from time to time on a national basis, using the knowledge that nature taught him, as with his winter moles, but generally speaking, he cannot expect plants and his friends in the animal world to interpret conditions in the south of England or Scotland, where weather conditions might be entirely different from those in Yorkshire.

His knowledge of natural phenomena can, however, be applied anywhere in the British Isles. The scarlet pimpernel will behave exactly the same in Devon and in North Yorkshire, if rain threatens, and so will the behaviour of other plants and animals.

Bill lays down the ground rules, as it were, and leaves it to the man-in-the-street to interpret them according to conditions in his own area, and in effect, become his own weather forecaster.

"I like to think of people doing this," he says. "It's a fascinating hobby, and encourages more and more people to take a personal interest in the mysteries of nature."

The only times he uses nature to form a national prediction, are when conditions such as major droughts or freeze-ups apply countrywide.

For his local forecasts, he has relied on a combination of the natural world, wind direction, and his ancient aneroid barometer, given to his parents as a wedding present in 1912. Sunsets played an important part.

A fiery red sundown, if high up, is a good sign, but if low down, the prospects are not so, he contends. A pinkish flush in the sky is a sure sign of fine weather the following day.

Cumulus clouds spell snow in winter, and thunderstorms in summer. Nowadays, because of his poor eyesight, he has to rely mostly on the barometer, with the help of Mrs Cook, although nature can still communicate certain information, such as if he finds himself in the middle of a swarm of craneflies, and interprets this as a sign that rain is in the offing.

He learned from his father that a barometric slow fall from high to low indicated wet weather with little wind. A rapid fall meant that strong winds were on the way.

When the barometer fell during low temperatures in winter, snow was often on the way. A slow rise from low to high was a sign of fine weather, possibly accompanied by high winds, whereas a rapid rise denoted the approach of unsettled weather.

Isobars, fronts and weather maps have never meant much to Bill. He doesn't pretend to understand strato-conflicts between high and low pressure. "All I need to know about atmospheric pressures is here," he says, giving 'old faithful' a tap.

W R Mitchell, a former editor of the prestigious Yorkshire magazine, The Dalesman, hit the nail on the head when he wrote in the Bradford Telegraph & Argus in 1995, "My favourite weather forecaster is not one of the professionals, with their television manner, computer graphics, and talk of isobars and fronts, but a cheerful octogenarian, Bill Foggitt of Thirsk, who has become famous for his predictions.

"He does his best, using a combination of family records; aspects of natural history, and current sightings.

"Each morning he glances across from his home to the spire of the parish church in the distance. Binoculars are used. If he can see the spire it's a good start, because he wants to consult the church's weathervane."

Bill smiled as he recalled the article. "No chance of doing that now," he reflects ruefully. "These days I can't even see the church, let alone its weathervane."

However, wind direction and speeds have, and still do, to a certain extent, play a notable part in his assessments, At least his loss of sight doesn't preclude him from telling him which way they are blowing - an excellent indicator of what conditions to expect.

Several years ago, he told a Daily Mirror feature writer that while working in Birmingham, where the concrete canyons confused wind direction, he would sniff the air, and if it carried the unmistakable aroma of chocolate, he knew it was crossing the Cadbury factory to the south west. That usually spelled rain.

If, on the other had, he caught the whiff of spicy pickles, the breeze was coming from the north east, where there was a sauce factory, and this, more often than not, indicated dry, if cold, weather.

If the smell of hops lingered in the air, the currents were undoubtedly transporting the effusion from a brewery. Bill laughed at his inability to recall where the brewery was in relation to his workplace, but went on, "That aroma quickly dispelled all thoughts of where the wind was coming from."

Well, if Bill had a good nose for what was in the wind, the Mirror man had an equally good nose for a story, and full-blown feature was the result.

Most people know about moist westerly winds and dry easterlies. They are also aware of the rain-bearing properties of the south westerly, and generally assume that zephyrs from the south are warm.

They may even have heard the ancient country rhyme: When the wind is in the east; tis good for neither man nor beast; when the wind is in the west, that is when it's at it's best; the north wind doth blow, and we shall have snow; when the wind is in the south it blows the bait into the fish's mouth.

Bill admits he cannot see the reasoning behind the reference to the south wind. In November 1997 it brought an almost record amount of rain to Yorkshire, but on the other hand, can be so dry that it carries what is believed to be sand from the Sahara to this country, to the chagrin of car owners.

In summer, Bill's weather-spotting is mainly confined to easterlies and westerlies; in winter he is concerned with winds coming from the north east, north and north west, all of which can be snow-laden. He also keeps a wary eye on south easterlies, which, although infrequent harbingers of snow, occasionally catch Yorkshire unawares, bringing blizzards as they sweep over low-lying Lincolnshire - straight up into the Vale of York, the "soft underbelly" of the county.

It is the north easterlies that bring the most vicious snowstorms to the area, which is most fortunate to have the protection of the great bulk of the North York Moors across its north eastern flank.

Although the highest point is less than 1,500 feet, they take the brunt of the onslaught, and are often cut off. To the south, the Yorkshire Wolds rise to only 800 feet, yet between them these two hilly areas guard the plain as if they were twice as high.

Nevertheless, Bill, who lives in the plain, knows that whenever particles of dry snow patter against the north east wall of South Villa, there is often trouble in store.

Thirsk itself usually escapes the worst of the storms, but five miles to the east, Sutton Bank, which is less than 1,000 feet above sea level, can quickly be blocked by huge drifts, making the road impassable.

Outside winter, Bill is accustomed to winds from the north and east being mainly dry and chilly, although gales can often accompany those from the north east.

The most unpopular wind in Yorkshire is undoubtedly the easterly, and he knows only too well that once established, it can blow constantly for weeks on end. A grey blanket of cloud usually covers the county, and great cracks appear in the soil as it dries out the land.

Yorkshire folk, Bill included, describe it as a "lazy" wind, because it is usually no more than a breeze, it gives no respite, and tends to go through, rather than round people.

In summer, east winds are the curse of the seaside holiday trade, for although they are often accompanied by bright sunshine for long periods, they also usher in the dreaded sea frets around early afternoon.

These dank walls of mist roll in from the North Sea, often reaching far inland, rapidly emptying beaches, but bringing smiles to the faces of amusement arcade owners, publicans and cafes. It's an ill wind ... they say.

Under normal conditions the prevailing winds are from the west; warm and rain-bearing. However, much of the moisture is deposited on the Pennines and the far west of Yorkshire, whereas by the time the clouds have drifted across to the East, they are breaking up, and consequently East Yorkshire is much drier.

Said Bill, "It's no coincidence that adders are more in evidence on the North York Moors than the Pennines. The drier it is, the better for them."

All these winds have their own character, and over the past 50 years, Bill has become adept at interpreting what each portends.

When it comes to global warming, Bill keeps an open mind. He cannot argue with the world's scientists, and accepts that things may be 'hotting up." He can accept the "greenhouse" theory, caused by gross pollution of the atmosphere.

But he believes that, being a man-made phenomenon, it is not a natural event, such as if the sun were getting hotter, or the earth's axis had started to "wobble," as it has done periodically since the earliest astronomical times. "We have had hot and cold cycles for thousands of years, and I think it is likely that we are in one of these," he added.

At any rate, he is not convinced that natural disasters will be any worse than those logged by his ancestors.

He recounted some of the extremes which regularly highlight his records since the first half of the last century.

In 1836, a few years after Bill's great grandfather, Thomas Jackson Foggitt, started his weather statistics, he wrote in his journal about a terrible snowstorm at Christmas, which engulfed the London to Edinburgh stagecoach not for from Thirsk.

Heroic attempts were made to extricate the carriage, but in the end it had to be abandoned, and the passengers taken to Thirsk, where they were accommodated in the Golden Fleece hotel.

Nothing could be done for the horses, however, and in an emotional final act, they had to be shot.

Yet, for many years the Vale of York has seldom seen more than a covering of snow.

On more than one occasion in mid-century, during the time of Charles Dickens, his entries referred to the icing over of the River Thames, particularly during the great freeze-up of 1840, when droves of skaters took to the ice.

On Christmas Day, 1860, the entry in his journal noted that the previous night, the temperature in his garden at Sowerby fell to zero, and had only risen by eight degrees during that day.

The weight of snow had snapped off a number of tree branches, and all the evergreen trees in the garden had been killed.

On Boxing Day he recounted how Disraeli's secretary walked home from Hyde Park, with his beard covered by icicles, adding that a man had collapsed and died in Thirsk market place as a result of freezing temperatures.

But it was his son, William (Bill's grandfather), who recorded the coldest January of all, in 1881. The average temperature for the month was 12 degrees below normal, while night temperatures fell below average on 29 occasions. Daytime temperatures failed to rise above freezing point on 14 separate days.

As if that wasn't enough, blizzards raged on no fewer than five days.

The Tay Bridge disaster in 1879 is referred to elsewhere in this book.

June 1887 was hot, dry - and parched. In fact the month of Queen Victoria's jubilee went by without any measurable rainfall being recorded in Thirsk, which William explained was a record as far as the family archives were concerned.

The winter of 1895 remains one of the severest on record, and was a talking point in the Foggitt family for years afterwards. Bill recalled hearing animated discussions about it - and he wasn't born until 1913.

Temperatures in January of that year were 8.7 degrees below average, and fell still further in February to a nadir of 11.3 degrees. Even in March, 1.5 degrees of frost took their place in the record book, and one of Bill's aunts, who was born that winter, used to joke that she had never been warm since.

Hot, dry summers were logged in 1899, 1900 and 1901, and of course, these were followed by long periods of heavy rain.

In October 1903, one of the wettest on record, normal rainfall was exceeded by seven inches, rounding off one of the coldest and wettest summers ever recorded by the family.

In 1905, the River Ure, in Yorkshire, froze over, allowing people to skate from Ripon to Boroughbridge.

Bill remembers listening in awe as his father, who was a chemist's assistant in London at the time, described the summer of 1911, when he saw flowers wilting before his very eyes in August, while walking in St.. James Park, such was the heat.

He added, "In Thirsk, my grandfather recorded 90 degrees on the same day."

By way of contrast, 1912 was so wet that Thirsk's picturesque little river, the Codbeck, burst its banks, and Bill believes it was this particular year when the floods were blamed for an outbreak of typhoid fever in the town.

The coldest night ever recorded was during the "soldiers' winter" of 1917, when 32 degrees of frost were logged for April 1st. It sounds almost like an April Fools Day joke, but Bill has the data to prove it. As if the men in the trenches didn't have enough to put up with!

In 1921, there was a 100-day drought, but in 1924, Bill recollects the downpours not only for their intensity, but because, appropriately, the popular song, It Ain't Gonna Rain No More, was released.

While he was at boarding school in Scarborough in February 1929, the weather was so cold that football was ruled out (to Bill's relief), so he went for a stroll on the beach, and was reduced to tears by the sights of scores of corpses of seabirds, mainly cormorants, which had frozen to death. The mean temperature for the month was seven degrees below average.

One of the most waterlogged summers recorded was in 1930, when the Codbeck transformed lower Thirsk into a lake, which led to the pithy remark from his friend, Leslie Hayes, a probationer Methodist minister who had just arrived in the town, "You didn't tell me Thirsk was so like Venice."

Another case of extremes "breeding" extremes was in 1933, when a ferocious blizzard swept across the North York Moors, piling up snowdrifts on Sutton Bank, near Thirsk, to depths of 40 feet.

And yet, two days later, Bill and his parents were setting off in a chauffeur-driven car, to visit his brother, who was at the same boarding school in Scarborough he had attended, and their way lay over the Bank.

They were taking a big chance. Huge drifts still loomed menacingly over the upper reaches of the 1 in 4 gradient, but the vehicle made it, to the astonishment of a policeman on duty at the summit.

Said Bill, "Presumably he thought anyone who could get up the bank was also capable of ploughing through to Scarborough, and he waved us on. We were the first motorists to get through after the blizzard and great credit was due to the driver."

He added, "Although it wasn't as long-lived as the great storm of 1947, it was almost as severe, but, just as in 1947, it was followed by a real scorcher of a summer.

In 1931, shortly before he left school, the rather cold and dismal summer was enlivened in the early hours of June 1st by a disturbance beneath the sea at Scarborough. It caused a violent tremor, which was felt as far inland as the West Riding, and along the coast to Ramsgate in Kent.

Although there were no reports of anyone being injured, a good deal of damage was caused to property.

Like many other people, Bill was alarmed when the earth trembled. He said his father recorded that the 12-second tremor at South Villa was followed by a sudden gust of wind which swept through the house.

The driest succession of summers was in 1932, 1933, 1934 and 1935, but 1938 was described by the 'Times' meteorological correspondent as "without peer" during the previous 50 years for its variety of atmospheric extravagance. Every month had been marked by eccentric behaviour of one kind or another. Presumably, sunspot activity was at its height that year, because, as Bill recalled, "For myself, the great thrill of 1938 was watching from the High Street in Biggleswade on the night of January 25th, the finest auroral display this century, seen not only from all parts of this country, but even as far south as Madeira.

"Astronomers tell us that particularly brilliant displays occur at times of maximum sunspot activity, and the larger the spots, the more spectacular the aurora."

It was in December 1946 that nature warned the Foggitts of what was to come.

During a mild Boxing Day, Bill's father pointed out a flock of waxwings, feeding on berries in their garden. He explained that they were visitors from Scandinavia, seeking refuge from the weather in their own country, adding that if the wind got round to the north east, they would be in for trouble.

"How right he turned out to be," said Bill. "By February the worst blizzards of the century had brought the country to a standstill. We were still recovering from the war, when we were devastated by the sheer weight of snow, which lasted until well into March. There have been colder winters, but none this century quite so vicious."

Compared with 1947, the cold winters of 1940 and 1941 were mere curtain-raisers.

Significantly, 15 and 16 years were to pass before the next really severe winters. These were in 1962 and 1963, the latter proving more intense. The north experienced 77 days of unremitting cold, and January was the coldest for 50 years, with a mean temperature 8.5 degrees below average at Thirsk.

And yet even this was milder than 1881.

However, 1964 was far milder, once again bearing out the Foggitt three-year theory. One of the mildest Januaries of recent years was in 1974, when mean temperatures were 2.5 above average.

The Foggitt family had a lucky escape in September 1965 when, for the first time since they moved to South Villa, the house was struck by lightning, which blew up the telephone.

Fortunately they were out at the time, because the telephone engineer later told them that anyone standing near the instrument could have been killed.

The fearful fury of the elements was felt throughout a wide area in July 1968, the year Bill first appeared on television. His mother, who was sitting in the bay window, called out, "Look at this black cloud coming towards us." By the time Bill got to her side, day had turned into night; everything went chilly, and the wind rose to a demonic howl.

Mrs Foggitt, who was 86 at the time, and a keen weather-watcher, swore she had never experienced anything like it in her life.

The tempest which probably lasted for about ten minutes, swirled on its path of destruction, leaving behind masses of branches, torn from their garden trees. Said Bill, "It was then that we realised that we had been through something of an 'American' experience, although on a considerably smaller scale. However, it served to remind us of the terrifying ordeals American citizens go though during the tornado and hurricane seasons, and how right we are to take note of 'breeding' conditions.

"Apparently it had been exceptionally hot in the south the day before, and the storm was caused by the collision of warm air from the south west, and cold currents from the north east - a veritable clash of Titans."

The prolonged heatwave of 1976 has been well-documented. Suffice it to say that Britain realised for the first time how precious - and limited - its water supplies were. Prayers were offered up in some areas for rain; hills and meadows turned brown; many factories learned to recycle their water - and, for the first time, the drought led to the active consideration of a national water grid.

For Bill, it was the first time a sunspot enabled him to predict a change.

"I was studying the setting sun one evening in August, when I noticed a conspicuous dot to the right of its centre, and bearing in mind what my father had told me, I deduced that a welcome change was at hand.

"Sure enough, by the end of the week, the heatwave was breaking up; the skies opened, and rainfall during September reached record levels. It never stopped all month, proving once again that in many cases, extremes lead to extremes.

"Mind you," he went on, "even this barely alleviated the effects of the drought, which would last for some years."

Outstanding in his memory is the time he was contacted by a Consett, County Durham, man, who had cut down a beech tree, and by counting its rings, had worked out that it was 120 years old. He had also noticed that the ring for 1889 was wider that the others. Had Bill any records that would account for this?

Bill had, and was able to inform his correspondent that the spring of 1889 had been one of the warmest on record. In addition to this, it was accompanied by abundant rainfall. Temperatures had been seven degrees higher than average.

For the sage, this finding represented a new dimension in analysing the weather.

All these facts have helped to show how supremely important the dedication of his forebears has been to Bill, who, of course, has contributed a great deal to the records himself.

Relying on his barometer and "secrets" of nature has ensured that, by and large, Bill's forecasts have been pretty accurate, and although he doesn't claim to be any sort of meteorological Moses, he has certainly been a pioneer in encouraging people to re-discover the lost art of assessing the weather.

Ever since those far-off Sunday afternoon walks with his parents, he has divined that the sensitivities of plants, animals and insects are attuned to nature's wavelength, to a degree beyond the understanding of most humans.

And in spite of modern scientific explanations of the various phenomena, he believes a lot of research still remains to be done in this field.

For instance, he found out about the instincts of field mice, which used to abound in the fields around his home, when they infiltrated South Villa before the onset of cold weather. "We would find them inside well before we realised we were about to be struck by an icy blast," he explained. "In fact, before one particularly cold spell, we had quite an invasion.

"Now I quite like these furry little creatures, probably because they are at the mercy of so many predators, but when I found one sharing my bed, I decided, reluctantly, that the time had come to get rid of them.

"They were creating a terrible noise, scurrying round the timbers during the night, and we never knew when we might have them for company at mealtimes. Even the cat's presence didn't seem to deter them, so it was time to call in the rodent inspector.

"I remember at that time carrying a pot with a 'strawberry' lid on it through to Betty Cook, but when I peered inside, a fieldmouse met my gaze. I was so surprised, I dropped the lid and it broke.

"But I wouldn't set traps for them, because I hate to think of these vulnerable little creatures suffering agony through being caught by a leg or the tail. After all, they did me a service by indicating that bitter weather was on the way.

"Nowadays, with factory units all round, there are considerably fewer of them."

As a point of interest, he recalled watching a mouse nibbling the cheese in a trap, set by someone else, and waited for the inevitable clunk. "But it didn't happen, so whether the trap was faulty, or that mouse was super-sensitive, I just don't know." He remembers this incident, because it happened on one of the rare occasions Win spent the night at South Villa.

He turned his attention to plants.

"Many of these are excellent allies of the amateur weather-diviner, as well as being very convenient if you know where to find them, for unlike animals and birds, they stay in one place."

He listed the scarlet pimpernel, found on roadsides, and known as the "poor man's weatherglass"; Welsh poppies; wood anemones; gentian; the humble chickweed, and a species of hawkweed known as "John-go-to-bed-at-noon."

"All these close their petals when rain is on the way, although John-go-to-bed-at-noon shuts up shop at lunchtime, whatever the weather, and I think this definitely calls for some scientific research. I have often studied the scarlet pimpernel, and every time its petals have closed, I have waited for about an hour before the onset of a shower."

He said he had been told that the reason for plants closing their petals was because they were protecting their pollen, adding that this explanation seemed entirely feasible.

"I was once able to point out this phenomenon when I appeared on 'Tomorrow's World' in the midlands, using Welsh poppies as an example.

"On the other hand, the evening primrose doesn't seem to like the sun or bright light, hence its name, and opens up in the evening, preferably when it's cloudy.

"On a slightly different tack, but still dealing with instinctive behaviour, I have experimented with foxgloves, tying them up against a wall in my garden. To my surprise, when I returned after a reasonable length of time, I found that they had twisted their heads round to face the direction from which insects were approaching.

107

"Here was an example of the symbiotic relationship between plants and the flying insects they obviously needed to carry out their pollination. It certainly makes you wonder at the intelligence, or instincts, of plants, which is, of course, taken to ultimate lengths in the case of the carnivorous Venus fly-trap, or sundew."

Because of this, added Bill, he never sneered at gardeners who talked to their plants. "And Prince Charles (who famously admitted he, too, conversed with his flowers) may not be so daft, after all."

Bill first arrived on the television scene with his pine cones and seaweed, and thirty years later, still maintained that these were among the best-known of nature's weather analysers.

Many urban dwellers, probably living on the edge of the countryside, like to impress visitors with their knowledge of nature by telling them how their pine cones open their scales in warm weather, and close them when it's wet and windy, but Bill doubts whether they understand why.

Young cones, he explained, had two or more winged seeds at the base of each scale, and it was these they were protecting when they closed up in wet, windy weather. When conditions were dry and mild, they opened, allowing the seeds to disperse.

For a long time after the seeds had gone, he added, the cones continued to react as if they were still under their protection.

"A woman once asked me why her pine cone never closed up - and then disclosed that she kept it hanging by her fireplace!"

As for the seaweed, he said it owed its forecasting ability to its hygroscopic salts, which made it damp and clammy when rain was in the atmosphere, but crispy in fine weather.

An example of the sensitivity of birds to changes in the weather occurred during a trip to the Lake District with friends.

"We were experiencing a heatwave, and the heat was enervating. Even the birds and animals appeared to be semi-comatose. One night, however, I was unable to sleep, not because of the humidity, but because the domestic birds were making such a racket."

Bill continued, "The closest parallel that comes to mind is the tale of the alarmed geese alerting ancient Rome to the proximity of the Gauls. I thought 'those birds know something I don't, and deduced that the hot spell was about to come to an end.

"Sure enough, in the morning the rain came surging in, and another lesson had been learned."

Swallows and house martins are also useful, both as long range and short range "forecasters." Bill normally expects to see them arrive about the middle of April, but if they show up before this, a fine, warm summer can be expected. "It may have something to do with the weather they have experienced earlier in their journey, but I cannot substantiate this," he admitted.

"In this district, I have noticed that these birds usually depart on or about October 4th, but if they fly off earlier, it is a good sign that autumn is going to be unsettled."

He went on, "I always feel quite sad, and, I must admit, a trifle envious, when I see these friendly little creatures congregating on telegraph wires, ready for their long journey to a warmer climate.

Another saying which has given me food for thought is the one which affirms that 'when rooks and gulls twirl in the sky, it's certain that a gale is nigh.'

"And kestrels, when they hover low, are believed to be hunting mice and other small mammals before rain and blustery weather, which inhibits them, sets in.

"One old saying that I place great store by is, 'better a wolf in the foldyard, than a farmer in shirt sleeves in January.' A mild January is usually followed by wintry weather in spring, when it is least wanted, and poses a real threat to sheep and lambs which have been put out to graze."

Some of Bill's favourite interpreters are frogs and moles ... the latter pursuing worms and grubs to the surface when a thaw is on the way, and in droughty conditions when the hard ground is about to be softened by rain.

Frogs also seem to know something we don't, when they spawn in the deepest part of a pond, or in the shallows. In the first case this presages a warm, dry spring, when deep water is the last refuge for emerging tadpoles; in the second, nearer the bank seems safe, because wet conditions are anticipated.

Both these forms of behaviour seem logical enough, and Bill has always been confident he could rely on it.

Just as obvious is when sheep or cattle huddle together when stormy weather threatens, or when sheep move off the moors in anticipation of snow.

We may, or may not be aware from the shelter of our cars, but to a farmer of old, it was signs like these that he was forced to rely on, as scientists at Reading University recognised, when they drew up a special project, including a section on the virtues of observation.

The hurricane of 1987 may have eluded Michael Fish, who has still not been allowed to forget it, but Bill says he knew that exceptionally high winds were on the way, because his cat, Blackie, went into a frenzy of activity, leaping onto walls, outhouse roofs, and windowsills.

The winds did lash Yorkshire, but caused nothing like the havoc they wreaked in the south.

Insects also play their part in foretelling changes. Bees loathe rain, and give ample warning of storms by disappearing into their hives, hence the saying, 'when bees crowd into the hive again, it's a sure sign of mist and rain.' Country lore also observes that, 'a swarm of bees in May, is worth a load of hay.'

Grasshoppers are also sensitive to advancing rain, "chirping" particularly noisily, and an old contention has it that house crickets (which are related) do the same. But who has house crickets on the hearth in these days of central heating?

Bill quoted two adages which his father used to impart, 'lazy fly, rain is nigh', and 'swift moves the ant when the mercury rises,' maintaining that both were accurate. "Just note how soporific flies become when thundery weather approaches. They attach themselves to human clothing, and can easily be swatted. And just watch ants scurry as it becomes warmer.

"Moths, too, seem to become lethargic when the atmosphere is heavy. I was in my sitting room one day, when I noticed what I later learned was a garden tiger moth, on the light fitting. Then it slowly fluttered down and settled on my wrist.

To my astonishment, shortly afterwards, the skin began to go red and swell, and at first I thought it must have bitten me, although I didn't see how it could have done this. At any rate, it caused me so much pain that I thought of calling the doctor.

"I have since read that this particular moth - I believe it was the garden tiger variety - is capable of inflicting a nasty rash."

It was during the great drought of 1976, while walking through the fields opposite his home, that Bill found himself among a cloud of craneflies, quite harmless insects, and his father's words about such a gathering presaging rain came back to him, adding ammunition to his sighting of the sunspot.

The rains duly came ...

Spiders, too, are useful to the amateur forecaster, if he can be bothered to study their webs. Bill has done so. "When spiders spin long radial strands, a spell of dry weather can be expected. It seems they know when such conditions are on the way, because they have the confidence to build wide, flimsy webs.

"When wet, windy weather is imminent, they spin short strands."

Other snippets of country knowledge observe that as long as the blackthorn flower lasts, we shall have cold, unsettled weather, while another bush which relishes wintry weather is, as its name suggests, the winter flowering jasmine.

When the weather starts to warm up, this shrub begins to shed its flowers. Said Bill, "I was told by my friend, the retired headmaster, that plants like this were brought back from Himalayan regions (or similar cold areas) by early British explorers, and because of this, could only flourish in this country in wintry conditions."

There are, of course, hundreds of these old sayings; many based on fact; several completely lacking in credibility.

Bill, for instance, completely discounts the popularly-held theory that a profusion of berries in autumn presages a cruel winter, because nature is giving the birds the chance to stock up, contending that all it shows is that spring was relatively frost-free, allowing unrestricted pollination.

He is much more prone to pay heed to the adage, 'when squirrels early start to hoard, winter will pierce us like a sword.'

However, if you think all this sounds like a walk in wonderland, one prestigious scientific organisation was to take the Foggitt saga only too seriously ...

Bill's finest hour was at hand.

For one day in 1993, a representative of Reading University appeared on his doorstep, and a bemused weatherman was informed that his observation of nature would be of great value to a new publication by the Association for Science Education.

The textbook, she explained, to be entitled, "Remote Sensing in Science Education," was destined to become a standard work in the national science curriculum.

The project was to be spearheaded by Professor J.K. Gilbert, head of the university's Department of Science and Technology Education.

Needless to say, Bill, who was then aged 80, stood there dumbfounded, and at first wondered if he were being set up for some student hoax. It took a lot of serious explaining from the academic emissary before the sage of South Villa was convinced she was genuine.

Television appearances and newspaper articles had always ben interested in his entertainment value, with some exceptions. But to be recognised as someone with an academic point to make was something he had never anticipated in his wildest dreams.

He cast his mind back to that heady occasion. "I realised I was about to be transported into an entirely new dimension, and found the experience exhilarating. I spent a lot of time explaining various aspects of folklore and sayings, and how my family and I had gone about our studies of nature's mysteries.

"She seemed fascinated."

Bill's contribution to the publication covered nearly three pages, under the heading, "Developing the Skills of Observation", and included a synopsis of the family tradition of record-keeping, headed, "The Foggitt Tradition of Weather Observations."

After the book was published, he commented, "It was a great honour to have participated, and I can say without reservation that this is the proudest moment of my life.

"I only wish my father could have been alive to witness my success. After all, he had so often hurt me by criticising my inability to master maths and science - yet here I was, the instigator of a large chunk of knowledge in a prestigious scientific journal.

"For a few delicious, self-deluding moments I felt I should have swapped my deerstalker for a mortar board but of course, the article also referred to observations by my forebears."

The section said the skills of accurate observation were a precursor to the development of remote sensing, which was described as the collection, storage, processing and display of data on the earth's surface; the near-earth environment, and space.

It went on, "Many folklore sayings, some based on observations, have been developed and passed down through the centuries. Some have been tested and found to have substance. Others have not.

"Selecting some of these sayings as a starting point in looking at how organisms react to changes in weather patterns, and how these old sayings respond to scientific investigation, provides a focus for developing observational techniques in the natural environment.

"The Foggitt family have made such observations, and kept detailed records of the reaction of animals and plants to the weather, and of weather patterns."

Later, Professor Gilbert described Bill as a "living legend," who was still practising methods of weather prediction used as long ago as the 15th century.

Quite an accolade.

CHAPTER 9

BANANA SKINS AND
A DISASTROUS LOVE AFFAIR

B ill has led what many people would consider an uneventful life, although he has sailed close to disaster on several occasions. He has known a succession of failures, emotional traumas, Sloughs of Despond, and ultimately success.

With his re-birth as a weather prophet, the dark clouds of uncertainty fell away, rather belatedly, at the age of 53. The peaks and troughs disappeared, giving way to settled conditions, his own home, and unalloyed happiness for more than 30 years.

He entered his new life, free of parental or marital restraint, re-vitalised in spirit. At last he was doing what came naturally to him.

However, while he closed the lid on Pandora's Box, he still couldn't help becoming involved in often embarrassing situations, some of them uncomfortable to say the least, but which he looks back upon with amusement at what he calls a "comedy of errors."

Many people have laughed with him - rather than at him - over his many escapades, which have only served to add spice to his reputation for being slightly eccentric, and in retrospect, no one chuckles more than Bill.

He lacks worldliness, and lives from day to day, never worrying about money (of which he has very little), which is often tucked into some obscure pocket, among fraying papers and letters.

He trusts in the Almighty, rather than timetables, for guidance, and views his "escapes" as miracles. He may be right at that, because although he has skidded on banana skins often enough, he has never done himself any lasting damage.

Since childhood he has always enjoyed going to church, especially when preaching. He loves the robust hymn singing; the simplicity of the church's message, and its custom of giving laymen responsibility for services.

In the past, some of these didn't have the advantage of a formal education, but were, nevertheless, extremely eloquent, Some, in their zeal, became virtual firebrands, but there was no mistaking their faith. Others had a natural sense of showmanship, and many, like Bill's great grandfather, would walk many miles to appear in a pulpit.

Bill recalls one young preacher who walked 12 miles from Ripon to deliver his message at Thirsk. It was a hot day, and on the way he stopped to eat his packed sandwiches. Little did he realise at the time that he was sitting on an ant-infested grass verge.

When he arrived at the chapel, the angry ants finally found a way through his clothing, and when he got into the pulpit, the congregation was startled to see him scratching furiously. He then exclaimed, "Friends, I have the word of God in my heart, but the devil's in my breeches."

Bill couldn't imagine anything so earthy interrupting the dignity of an Anglican service!

Another incident involved a flamboyant local preacher, who believed in putting his words into actions. So when he talked about the ease with which a person could fall from grace, he promptly slid down the pulpit bannisters, while to illustrate the difficulty of returning to faith, he crawled back up the steps.

Bill grinned at the recollection. "My mother, an Anglican, happened to be at that service. She sniffed at this demonstration, and said it was only showmanship. And so it might have been, but it certainly got the point across."

Another story, which he admitted might be apocryphal, but had it on good authority, concerned a blind Methodist minster, whose congregation on a day of appalling weather, consisted of just one person - an elderly lady who was partially deaf.

The minister's address included the account of Jacob's encounter with the angel, shortly before he changed his name to Israel. The quotation (taken from the Methodist hymn book) went thus, "With thee all night I mean to stay, and wrestle till the break of day."

Unfortunately the woman, in her deafness, thought the preacher was referring to her, and outraged, stormed out of the building, saying, "Oh no, you won't - I'm going," leaving the minister totally nonplussed.

An embarrassing occurrence in Bill's own chapel happened when a former minister, who was castigating sharp practice, giving the watering down of milk as an example, was interrupted by a local milkman, who begged him, "Stop, stop - you're giving me palpitations!"

To which the man of God replied, "Well, if the cap fits, wear it."

With that the man promptly absented himself from the chapel, and never returned.

Said Bill, "I don't think the minister was accusing him personally of watering his milk, but he may have had a sense of guilt through association."

A daily pint of beer, or on special occasions a pint and a half, is something Bill refuses to do without, despite the traditional Methodist disapproval of strong drink.

He likes nothing better than to wind up his day's shopping with a visit to the Golden Fleece or Three Tuns hotels, for what he calls his "blood transfusion," while after preaching on a Sunday evening, a pint provides an "epitaph" to the service.

He said, "Most ministers I have known have been extremely tolerant of my 'weakness' and I can think of only one who manifestly disapproved. He passed away some years ago.

"As it happened I liked and respected him a lot. He'd been a dedicated missionary in the Gambia, along with his wife, and both were true pillars of the Methodist church.

"One Friday, he and I were attending a meeting of the Probus club in Thirsk, when he came across to where I was sitting, and said, 'Hello Bill, can we have a little chat?'

"I said I'd be delighted, but would just go and get my pint. When I returned from the bar, he'd gone.

"That empty seat spoke more than any words he could have uttered, and I must admit I felt a little guilty. But a pint of beer is one of my few pleasures. A retired Methodist minister who comes to see me now and then, always brings me a couple of cans of ale, and I used to have some wonderful conversations over a glass of beer with a retired circuit superintendent minister, the Rev Walter Mole.

"Sadly, Walter passed on a few years ago. I will always remember his for his sense of humour and tolerance." He added: "I jokingly tell the present minister that my taste for a pint is merely a thirst after righteousness."

The most unforgettable payment Bill received for an article came from a Financial Times writer, who turned in a particularly comprehensive piece about the background to his forecasting methods.

His face widened in a smile at the memory. "The next time I walked into the Three Tuns and asked for my usual pint, I was informed that it had been paid for, which, of course gratified me no end. But when the barman said there were plenty more to come, my bewilderment must have shown on my face.

"It turned out that the F T man had left enough to keep me in beer for something like two or three months. It was his way of saying 'thank you' for the information I'd given him, and was the most imaginative 'fee' I have ever received. He obviously had me pretty well weighed up, and I am still grateful when I think about it."

Nowadays Bill varies his pilgrimages between the Three Tuns and Golden Fleece hotels. He is warmly welcomed in both, but during the past year had had to cut down on his original two pints. "I get a bit dizzy after two", he explains.

115

On his eightieth birthday, the "magic circle" presented him with a handsome tankard, but this, unfortunately, was later stolen from the Three Tuns Hotel, probably, Bill believes, by a racegoer who spotted it under a table where he had put it, thinking it would be safe. "I am upset to this day about the mean theft of that drinking vessel," he mourned.

Members of the "magic circle" were on hand a few years ago when Bill slipped on the icy market place cobble stones while leaving the Three Tuns. He fell quite heavily, partially stunning himself, and his friends helped him back into the hotel foyer. One wag joked, "Well Bill, I could understand you being carried out - but never carried in."

Bill's contract with Yorkshire Television ended in 1983 after 15 years, and it was two years later that he "struck gold" with his famous "moles" prediction. It was time a commercial organisation, outside the realm of press and television, stepped in ...

It was about this time that a go-ahead British Telecom marketing executive in Middlesbrough hit upon the novel idea of putting Bill's forecasts on tape, and inviting subscribers to phone in on a special line to listen to them.

Bill was all for it, and the first day the service opened, Northallerton 779595 was deluged by more than 3,000 calls. Those who got through were greeted by the weatherman's cheerful voice announcing, "Hello, this is Bill Foggitt of Thirsk, giving you the weather forecast for July."

Soon BT were rushing in extra lines to cope with the demand. People, used to suave television broadcasters with their isobars and weather maps, listened agog as this homespun man informed them that, because June had been cold, prospects for July were much better.

He explained that large numbers of swallows and martins, and the midges on which they fed, indicated that the air was becoming warm and dry, and would remain so for the first half of the month.

Bill was "over the moon" when he was told there had been a congratulatory call from Australia, from a man who had heard about the novel phone-in, and had dialled Northallerton from the other side of the world to hear what he had to say.

Later, he was to appear on German television, informing eager viewers about some of his more unusual methods used in his predictions. Co-producer Robert Green said at the time, "Mr Foggitt is the sort of strong, interesting character we are looking for on this programme."

Thus it was that Bill came to sell his "secrets" to his former enemy.

In 1990 the English Tourist Board jumped on the bandwagon, in an attempt to persuade holiday makers of the attraction of winter breaks. They felt it would help their campaign if they propagated some of his folksy adages.

They produced a glossy brochure with the emphasis on these, typified by the following sayings, If the oak wears its leaves in October, it heralds a harsh winter. A cold November, warm Christmas. Thunder in December presages mild weather, although not necessarily fine. Better see a wolf in the foldyard, than a farmer in shirt sleeves in January.

Nor was this the last time the Board made use of Bill.

At the age of 80, the weatherman was walking across the forecourt of a Thirsk garage when he was knocked down by a car. "I felt a blow and finished up on my side," he said. "I was badly shocked, and memories of the 1966 accident flooded back, but luckily this time I was unhurt, just badly shaken.

"When I arrived at the hospital someone - I believe it was a nurse or an auxiliary - exclaimed, 'Why, it's Mr Foggitt isn't it? Is it going to be a white Christmas, Mr Foggitt?"

He grinned wryly. "I wasn't giving much thought to the weather at the time, as I remember, but I suppose she was only trying to cheer me up. Anyway, she was abruptly cut short by an ambulanceman, who told her curtly I had more important business at that moment than foretelling the weather."

Many of Bill's difficulties occurred in Helmsley, his favourite little town, 14 miles from Thirsk across the Hambleton Hills. Here it was that Audrey had whispered words of love to him, and the nostalgia still lingered all those years later.

His problems usually involved his black, crossbred terrier, Sambo ("I wouldn't be allowed to call him that nowadays, would I?"). Bill used to love taking the mischievous little fellow for walks along the banks of the River Rye, and through the magnificent ruins of Rievaulx Abbey, before calling in at the Black Swan for refreshment.

After one such invigorating stroll, he called in at the hotel for a bar meal and a pint, but after an extended wait for his food, asked a waiter what had happened. He replied, quite unconcernedly, that Sambo had bitten the waitress, and she'd "gone for a jab", but not to worry - she'd be all right.

Said Bill, "I was quite worried. I didn't know how badly the dog had bitten the waitress, and had visions of the hotel taking me to court - or even worse, barring me. Besides, I knew the waitress, who was a kindly person.

"Anyway, I was fortunate. Neither fate befell me, and I am sure it was all down to the goodwill of the woman. Can you imagine the kerfuffle that such an incident would have caused in some establishments?"

Sambo's next victim was a German tourist. It wouldn't have been too bad during the war, perhaps, but this happened in the genteel surroundings of the Feversham Hotel, in Helmsley. And the German was quite nice, actually.

"We were in the bar, when this large fellow with a bald head, plus-fours and a huge cigar, came in; saw the dog, and beamed, 'Ah, ein hund, ja?' I conceded this, but warned him not to attempt to stroke him.

"Perhaps he simply didn't understand. He repeated, 'Nice hund, ja?' and bent down to pat him. Sambo promptly bit him on the leg.

"I'll not forget what happened in a hurry," Bill went on. He let out a startled shout. His cigar went flying, and looking stunned, he slumped into an armchair to examine his leg.

"I told him I was very sorry, but pointed out that I had warned him. Then Sambo and I made an undistinguished exit from the hotel. Again I was lucky. I never heard anything more about the incident. Perhaps as well as not understanding English too well, the gentleman didn't know our laws for keeping dogs under proper control. Or maybe he didn't consider himself bitten badly enough to pursue the matter."

Bill's terrier certainly had a mind of his own, and obviously didn't take too kindly to being tied to a drainpipe, while his owner gossipped inside a Helmsley shop.

Whatever, when Bill eventually emerged, there was no Sambo - and no drainpipe.

It took 20 minutes of frantically searching the market place, before he came across him, wagging his tail, and trailing a long piece of downspout behind him.

Once, however, he go really angry with Sambo. "I had taken him for his usual stroll by the River Rye," he said, "when we were overtaken by torrential rain. Just then the dog decided it would be fun to chase cows in an adjoining meadow. I yelled and yelled at him to come back, but he took not the slightest notice, so I decided to scale the barbed wire fence and grab him by the collar.

"That was a terrible mistake. I must have been well into my sixties, and inevitably I got stuck. Pinioned, what's more, in an extremely vulnerable place. In fact I realised that if I tried to extricate myself, those wicked metal prongs could do my masculinity severe damage.

"The rain was still coming down in bucketsful. Sambo, totally oblivious to my plight, was still careering about after the cows, and I began to think I would have to spend the night impaled on the fence. I thought about that sergeant-major in Palestine, bellowing about being hung on the wire at Mons.

"I was, quite literally, on the horns of a dilemma. It occurred to me that I could even die of exposure. Talk about Worzel Gummidge!

"I was in despair, when suddenly I saw two girls walking along the footpath. I heard one exclaim, 'Look, a scarecrow. There wasn't one here the last time I came! Then getting closer, she recognised me as having given a recent talk to the local young farmers club. 'Why it's Mr Foggitt,' she called to her companion. 'What's he doing here?'

"She may have said something about me catching me death of cold, and when I explained my predicament, they were briskness itself. They told me not to worry, they would run back to the farmhouse and get a pair of scissors.

"In fact they did better than that. They also brought a spare pair of trousers. The scissors, I must say, were huge - more like a pair of shears, and that set me thinking along a different tack. What it they slipped? And what if the girls accidentally exposed me?"

"But I needn't have worried. Those girls were typical country lasses. Practical and confident. Snip, snip, went the scissors, and suddenly the pressure from that awful fence eased.

"I slipped discreetly into the pair of trousers they had brought, and we set off back to the farmhouse for a welcome cup of tea. The girls told me I'd been lucky, because they seldom walked that particular path, especially on a rainy day.

The hospitality didn't end there, however. A member of the family even ran Sambo and I home. Those girls will be grown up women by now, but if they remember me, I would like them to know they still have my deepest gratitude."

Sambo got a roasting, but Bill didn't have the heart to bear a grudge for long.

But, inevitably, it was his canine companion who again caused problems. Once again they were walking along the Rye, when Sambo, who as usual had raced ahead, scrambled down a steep bank to where the water was quite deep and plunged in.

Bill was in a quandary. He was too old to get down the slope, which was too steep for the dog to be able to get any purchase. "He couldn't climb out, and kept falling back into the water. I began to panic, thinking he might drown, but just then salvation arrived in the form of a couple out walking.

As it happened I knew them. 'Don't worry, Mr Foggitt', shouted the young man, who saw what was happening, 'I'll have him out in a jiffy.' He slid down the bank, got a strong hand round Sambo's collar, and hauled him to safety, to my eternal gratitude.

However, I shudder to think what would have happened if Sambo had also shown his gratitude - by biting his saviour!

But the little terrier did have his uses, whatever his shortcomings, and redeemed himself one evening after Bill had attended a meeting of local preachers - at Helmsley, of course.

After the meeting, Bill was chatting to a friend, oblivious to the time.

"Sambo was barking furiously, and leaping up at me, and I was getting quite irritated, until suddenly it dawned on me that the last bus to Thirsk was on the point of departure. I bade my companion a hurried goodbye, and made a dash for it, just managing to scramble aboard while it was moving off, dragging Sambo behind me.

"As I sank into my seat, getting my breath back, the conductor grinned, and told me that if it hadn't been for my dog I'd have been spending the night in Helmsley."

Bill smiled as he re-lived the antics of his irrepressible friend, who died 11 years ago. "I really loved that dog. He was a true companion for me, even if he was occasionally naughty. In any case, it wasn't really the dog's fault. He had been treated very badly before he came to me, so it was no wonder he was touchy."

One of Bill's early mishaps, which foreshadowed several others, occurred after he had been invited to take part in a programme on BBC Radio Cleveland, at Middlesbrough.

Harry Whitton, a Thirsk author and humorist, accompanied him to the station, where the manager had promised to take them out to lunch.

But it just had to happen. Bill went out for a pre-lunch stroll; lost his way in a huge shopping centre, and failed to re-locate the BBC offices. While Harry and the manager were frantically telephoning the police and hospitals, he was wandering around a bewildering maze of shops, and finally turned into a cafe for a bowl of soup.

He did eventually manage to find his way to the station, but it was too late to be taken to lunch, and Harry, to his exasperation, had to settle for a ham sandwich.

Bill has a rather droll sense of humour on occasions. He had travelled to Scarborough, again with Harry, to attend a writers' circle meeting. Before it started, they went to the bar for a drink, but were none too enamoured of the barmaid's apparent indifference.

As she continued to stack bottles under the bar, Bill asked Harry in a stage whisper, "I wonder how much she charges for haunting houses." Harry quickly looked away as the woman fixed Bill with a look that would have driven rooks screaming from their nest.

Luckily for Bill, she didn't make any comment, but the embarrassed weatherman realised he'd probably gone too far. "After all," he conceded, "she was probably a very nice woman."

In 1985 he was invited by breakfast television to travel to London to be interviewed. He got the message just as he was about to leave to preach at a Methodist chapel in a village near Thirsk.

He rushed through his address, and just managed to catch the train to the metropolis.

But, as so often happens, haste led to confusion, and having arrived in London, what did he do but turn up at the wrong hotel. The television company told him they had booked him into a certain establishment, but Bill said later, "I got mixed up somehow. I must have known the hotel I finished up in, otherwise why would I go there?

"Having arrived, I was dismayed to find I had no reservation. I explained the circumstances, and the staff kindly telephoned the television company, but at that time of night there was no reply. I wandered into the bar, and was staggered to be told the price of a pint of beer was at least 60p more than I would have paid in Thirsk.

"The hotel manager, however, was a pretty decent sort of chap, and understood my dilemma. He offered to find me a room for the night if I would pay a deposit, but I hadn't even enough money for that, so, feeling rather disgruntled, I made my way to Kings Cross station, where I was fortified by the most delicious cheeseburger I had ever tasted.

"After that I had a tedious journey home, finally arriving at South Villa about 4 am - only to find that in my haste to change my clothes I'd mislaid my key, and was locked out.

"My only chance of getting in was through the kitchen window, which luckily was unlocked. What a struggle I had. I was aged 72 and not very active, and anyone seeing me wriggling about would have thought me the most incompetent of burglars.

"Naturally I became stuck. My legs were waving helplessly over the sink, and Sambo was barking furiously. He either didn't recognise the soles of my shoes, or was giving me encouragement.

"By the time I eventually managed to manoeuvre myself through, it was 5 am, so I decided it was too late to go to bed, and took Sambo for a walk instead."

He added, "When my friends read about my exploit in the local paper, I came in for quite a lot of gentle ribbing."

However, he was somewhat mollified when the television company expressed sympathy and reimbursed him.

Another "situation" featuring the intrepid weatherman occurred when a television company, anxious to lend "colour" to an interview, asked him to turn up in the guise of a country yokel.

Bill duly obliged, wearing a billycock, rough and worn tweed jacket and trousers tied up with string, boots and a cudgel. As it happened, there was a rail strike at the time, and he was forced to fly to London from Leeds/Bradford airport.

"You should have seen the looks I go when I got there. I must have looked like a character straight out of a Wessex novel, and sensed that passengers were thinking I'd missed my muck cart and landed up at the airport. They probably wondered, too, why I had the temerity to board the aeroplane.

"When I eventually arrived at the studio, the make-up experts painted some sort of a beard on me, and the interview went off quite satisfactorily.

"But then, as usual, things started to go wrong. Same old story, I thought, as a garrulous taxi driver took me to the airport, but had talked so much I missed the plane, which meant I had to book in at the airport hotel for the night.

"Can you imagine the looks of horror when I trudged into that swish establishment?"

The reception staff seemed to be saying, 'Who allowed that tramp to get into the building?'

And when I asked for a room they were speechless.

"It was obvious that they weren't going to allow me to stay, and heaven knows what I would have done, but the little miracle came, as if to order. At that moment another receptionist came in, looked at me, and exclaimed, 'Hello, Mr Foggitt, fancy seeing you here.'

"The rest of the staff were stunned. 'Do you know this man?' they asked. 'Of course,' she replied. 'It's Mr Foggitt, the weatherman. He's just been interviewed on television.'

"Well, you should have seen the change in their attitude. Suddenly they couldn't do enough for me, and when I got through to the bar, instead of being hustled out, the barman grinned and handed me a pint, saying, 'Get this down you - you'll feel like a new man.'

"Which, of course, I did.

"Hearing about my plight, the following day the television people had the goodness to send me all the way back to South Villa by taxi. I must say they know how to throw money about. I know it sounds improbable, but I believe this was yet another example of somebody up there looking after me. Thank goodness for that young receptionist."

Bill was again in trouble in the capital when he answered a Sky television request for an interview. "They told me a driver would be waiting for me at Kings Cross with a placard, but in the crowd I couldn't see him. He may have been there, but I wandered up and down the platform for at least half an hour without catching sight of him, so I decided to take a taxi to the studios.

"The driver informed me, however, that there were three locations for Sky, so I gave it up as a bad job and caught the next train home.

"I should have received a £75 appearance fee, but when a friend rang Sky to explain what had happened, they apologised and generously sent me £150. They said they had sent a driver to meet me, and couldn't understand what had gone wrong."

The unworldly weatherman was again in trouble following another excursion to London. This time he was booked in at one of the Hilton hotels, where there were mechanical drinks dispensers in the bedrooms.

To his astonishment, some time after his return, he received a bill for £7.41 for drinks from the machine.

He protested to a friend, "You know me - I never have anything to do with mechanical gadgets, because of the trouble they get me into. And in any case I never touch spirits. I had my usual pint in the hotel bar, and that was that."

The friend rang the Hilton to explain this, adding that Mr Foggitt was most upset by the demand. They said they would look into it, but Bill heard nothing more.

"By this time," he declared, "I was getting pretty fed up with going to London. I wasn't getting any younger, and decided not to go again."

But before he terminated his love/hate relationship with the capital, he was asked to make another appearance. It was one he could scarcely refuse, because it was to promote a new book, "Weatherwise," published by Pavilion Books in 1992, under his copyright.

So once again he found himself at York station, having a pre-journey drink in the bar of the then Royal Station Hotel, where he became so interested in a conversation he was having, that he completely forgot about the train. He said, "I suppose people would say that's typical of me, and I must admit to being a bit absent-minded. Anyway, I caught the next train, and by the time I arrived at Pavilion Books they were beginning to give me up.

"However, they welcomed me warmly, and after a drink, booked me into a hotel.

"The following morning at 6 am I was woken up by a sepulchral voice saying, 'They have come to take you away.' The interview was with morning television, who transported me to what looked like a cottage with a big garden, where they hoped to see some moles in action." It was pouring with rain, and I am sure that the interviewer who sat beside me on a bench had about nine-tenths of the protective umbrella. I got absolutely soaked, and was sure I would develop pneumonia.

"And to cap it all, we never did see any moles."

All these imbroglios paled into insignificance, however, beside his celebrated collision with a femme fatale in 1984.

This, probably more than anything else, exposed his trusting nature and naivete, as he was drawn into the clutches of a self-seeking woman.

The affair, if it could be so called, made a considerable hole in his pocket, and could easily have cost him his respected position within the Methodist church.

It all began with Bill selling several acres of land to the local council for industry, which, as stated previously, gave him the means to carry on living at South Villa.

He finished up with around £23,000 - an absolute fortune to him - and not unnaturally wanted to share his windfall with this friends.

Thus it was with "jingling pockets" and purposeful stride that he made his way to the Three Tuns hotel. He was the life and soul of the ensuing party , but, unbeknown to him, someone else was taking more than a casual interest in the way he was spending his money.

An acquaintance of Bill's had incautiously remarked to a woman hovering at the edge of the group, that he had sold a chunk of land, and as a result, was considerably well off.

The message was clear - and as soon as the opportunity arose, the unscrupulous female pounced.

She engaged Bill in conversation, and eventually started to flatter him. She described herself as a widow, although she was, in fact, a 46-year-old divorcee, and went on at length about an elderly man like him living alone. The innuendo would have been spotted immediately by any worldly- wise person - but not by Bill, who was quite carried away by her attentions and concern.

The sweet talk, fuelled by a few drinks, went to his head, and in due course led to a hotel bedroom, where they spent the night.

However, Bill later stressed that because of the amount of alcohol he had consumed, he went straight to sleep.

The following day (Sunday), they strolled arm-in-arm through Thirsk market place, and Bill even took her to a service in a village outside the town, where, he said, "Everything went deathly quiet when we walked in."

For two or three days he and his paramour were seen around Thirsk, and the second night was spent together in the former Royal Oak residential hotel, the besotted sage having spent hundreds of pounds on clothes and jewellery for her.

That afternoon, the couple were spotted sitting by the fireplace in the Royal Oak, and a friend approached them. After a few pleasantries, the woman turned to him and said, "Do you think Bill and I could make a go of it?"

He muttered a non-committal reply and returned to the bar, where a CID officer he knew whispered urgently , "For Christ's sake, try and get Bill away from that woman." He, apparently, knew all about her.

But how does one convince an infatuated 71-year-old that he's heading for the rocks? The simple answer is that you don't. Michael Hodgson, the then landlord of the Royal Oak said afterwards, "I saw them heading upstairs together and one of them dropped a sandwich which our Labrador, Tuppence, was quick to gobble up."

Some time during Monday or Tuesday, Bill even bought her an "engagement" ring - forgetting that he wasn't in a position to marry.

The police later stepped in and arrested the woman, who eventually finished up in crown court at Teesside.

Meanwhile, Thirsk was agog with gossip. Just about the whole town knew about Bill and his "girlfriend." People stopped him in the street to shake hands and congratulate him. The vicar of a parish outside Thirsk actually offered to marry them. Others shook their heads and said the whole thing would end in disaster - and they were right.

Bill himself was in a sort of daze. On one hand he could scarcely believe his luck; on the other, misgivings about where it was all going to end assailed him.

In fact it ended at Teesside crown court, where the woman admitted four charges involving deception, and was sentenced to three years' probation, the prosecution pointing out that she had previous convictions for similar offences.

The court was told that the defendant had entered into a three-day fling with Mr Foggitt, during which time there was an intense relationship. He bought her clothes and jewellery, and also an engagement ring. Later, she took one of his credit cards, and spend £150 before being caught.

The prosecutor added that she told police, "Bill's a gentleman, but you know me - I'm in a world of my own."

After the case, which led to a variety of weather-related headlines in the press, Bill insisted that he had behaved with absolute propriety throughout, and that nothing physical occurred.

He told friends he had drunk far too much, and had simply gone to sleep, which to anyone who knows the "inkling, twinkling, tiggywinkling sage of Thirsk," as Mike Amos, was years later to describe him in the Northern Echo, certainly rings true.

To me, personally, Bill confided, "I was in a daze most of the time, carried away by my good fortune, and then being flattered by an attractive brunette, who was much younger than me. They say there's no fool like an old fool, and this business certainly showed me that, no matter how old you may be, you never stop learning."

He added that everyone had been extremely supportive about the "affair," and the Methodist church "very understanding."

Then he perked up again. "Do you know, that as a result of the publicity the case received, I had a proposal of marriage from a lady in Cheshire? Needless to say I declined her kind offer."

But, almost as an afterthought, he mused, "When I think back, it was fun while it lasted."

And that, you could say, sums up Bill's attitude to life.

No matter how grey the skies, or how loud the thunder, always anticipate bright periods and have the Almighty as a companion.